Once Upon Our Childhood

Lara Brown

Published by Worlds via Words, 2020.

Once Upon Our Childhood
A novel by Lara Brown
Copyright © 2020 Lara Brown
Front cover art by Spark Creative

This is a work of fiction. Names, characters, places, and incidents are products of the author's imagination or are used fictitiously. Any resemblance to actual events or persons, living or dead, is entirely coincidental.

ISBN: 978-0-9888839-1-8

For Dad, Ma, Dee

those who first believed...

Part I: Ring a-ring o' roses, a pocket full o' posies

PROLOGUE

FOUR GIRLS SAT ON THE concrete ledge under the gum tree—two at each extreme end, creating a bracket around the other two in between. Three stood up slowly, one after the other, from the ledge and drifted away into the distance until she was alone, left behind hunched down on the right side of the ledge.

She looked down at her clenched fist, determined. This time, she was prepared. This time, nobody was going to stop her from drifting away into the distance too. She sat and waited, her fist still clenched.

After a long, unbearable moment of waiting, she saw him at last. Her monster with two faces, faces she had never seen, faces masked in chilling black silk.

She stood to face him. Her heartbeat pulsated loudly and rhythmically, as though along to the sound of an ukulele, as she and her monster squared away as they always did in a time-old dance. The dance of death.

He moved abruptly but did not catch her unawares this time. She moved too like lightning in the opposite direction. She tore through the night on a wild and empty landscape of nothingness, the cruel, acrimonious wind her other enemy as it pushed back against her as if in cahoots with the original enemy.

Even so, she persisted. There would be no victory tonight but hers. He was gaining ground, however. She made her first mistake when she looked over her shoulder to see how far behind he was, and her second when she tripped over her feet. She recovered but too late.

Cold hands grasped her arms and knocked her down. Her back to the ground, she stared up, the breath escaping forcefully through her pinched nostrils as her monster stood over her, the two masked faces leering.

He made to move but stopped in apparent confusion at the object lying in her now outstretched palm and the smile of victory playing on her face.

Did she think to attack him and live to tell the tale? She answered the voiceless question hanging in the air as her monster was suddenly drenched in spurting rich, red blood that was not his own.

...She woke up with a loud gasp, drenched in copious, tepid sweat. As she regained her bearings, her shoulders sagged in defeat and her hand clutched at her now aching heart.

Glancing over to the other side of the room, she slipped out of bed, careful not to make a single sound. Indeed, aside the slight creak of the bathroom door as it was pushed close gently and then, a second or two of rustling, not a sound could be heard...not really.

It was three in the morning but the ears of the half-asleep dogs downstairs pricked at the humming coming from one of the bathrooms upstairs. It was faint, quite faint, but there it was.

"...laugh, kookaburra, laugh. Kookaburra, gay your life must be." She was humming the rhyme as two silver buttons of tears escaped down her cheeks, as she expertly moved the edge of the razor from left to right on the exposed skin, as she winced at the sight of the dripping rich, red blood that was her own.

CHAPTER ONE

Lara

AT EIGHTEEN, MY FRIENDS and I struck everyone as your typical, run-of-the-mill teenagers—the invincible sort who thought the world their very own oyster, you know, who thought they knew everything there was to know about themselves, about each other, about everyone else around them, about life.

We are here to tell you how we faked that illusion by creating prettily embroidered stories of our individual lives and how each of those stories ripped apart at the seams at the same time. It was all once upon our childhood.

My name is Omolara Kharan, and I am the irascible daughter of Mr. Julius Kharan and Ms. Oluwadara Abbey (ex-Kharan, ex-Wilder). Cue mock applause for the love episode: Portugal meets Nigeria.

Now, this would have been the very mundane introduction to what would have been a very mundane story, had life not taken the wheel. What wheel, you say? Let me finish, will you!

If this were an elementary English composition class, I would be at liberty to describe in colorful detail the big, almond eyes which unequivocally do not reek of innocence, the long jet-black hair which has never seen fit to curl, the heart-shaped lips that have told one too many lies, etcetera, etcetera—all of which belong to me, of course.

Thankfully, this is not an English composition class and for all my many perceived flaws—She lies! She smokes! She drinks! She dresses like that renowned streetwalker in her heydays! She never listens!—I am not a braggart. Suffice it to say, I am one of the most beautiful people that I have ever met.

I recently turned eighteen and by my calculations, have spent roughly four years in this hellhole of a country getting to know the father and two brothers I never knew I had.

Stop.

Rewind.

So, four years prior, my mother, Dara Abbey, newly divorced from her second husband, James Wilder, had seen fit to yank me from the country I had always known as home—God bless America—because it was becoming alarmingly clear that she might have done a lousy job of raising the kid.

The kid in question had a mouth immune to antibacterial soap and a severe allergy to discipline and that, mind you, was putting it nicely. Some jail-time in the motherland (pun completely intended), Nigeria, would do the kid good, Ms. Abbey reasoned.

How could she have predicted that she would end up running into her first husband, the father of the kid, and her two older sons, the kid's brothers, in Lagos of all places? After all, she had left them in Amadora, Portugal a long time ago or so she had thought!

Well, what do you know? Dear Ms. Abbey was inevitably faced with the thankless task of briefing the hapless kid that um, you know, Daddy isn't so, um, dead after all. No, he isn't. In fact, he has got two living replicas of himself!

Yeah.

The peace has been some long tumultuous four years coming. Mother and father have partly reconciled their differences (or at least, appear to have done so for the sake of the kids), and sister and brothers have bonded tightly. The kids live with Mom one week and with Dad the next. It is not the typical one big happy family, but it will do.

Besides, the kid's potty mouth is not so potty anymore and the blazing Lagos sun did turn out to be a slight panacea for that allergy to discipline. So yes, while Omolara might not exactly be the perfect kid and probably never will be, but hallelujah, her soul just might have been saved from the devil.

Fast-forward.

Now that I have impressed on you my beauty and wit, let me tell you about my best friends. Folasade Adeyemi is sitting beside me with her tongue racing at 1,000,000 mph as it is wont to do. She is the one with the wide expressive eyes, atypical razor-thin lips, and a head full of black-brown hair.

If she were a couple of inches taller, Fola would be fielding questions all the time from overzealous folks as to why she was not a model. Not that I blame them—she walks with a formidable stride that lets you know darn well that she has always been on top of the world and will always be.

Miss 'Daddy-is-a-bloody-rich-telecommunications-mogul' is the most unabashedly spoilt horrors I have ever met in my lifetime and boy, that is not saying much! Her daddy obsessively makes too much money to make up for the time he never has for her, his mini-me son, Folasayo, and his consultant-manager wife.

Picture multiple properties on Banana Island alone and exotic trips abroad every single school holiday and you'll develop an acute understanding of what constitutes the rather boring norm in the Adeyemi household.

To be fair, her being unapologetically spoilt stems from her being a fragile and weak baby, albeit one who has grown up into this bossy, domineering but relatively naïve teen.

Still, I love her more than I love my adverbs. She is one of my best friends, so she must be getting at least one thing right. She was one of the first few friends I made when Mom and I first moved to Lagos, and I could never forget how open-heartedly she had embraced me despite how surly I had been in those early days.

I love the fact that she has the greatest sense of humor and that, like me, she is always up for anything over the top. She loves being in the thick of things, and she can also be compassionate and caring and loving...when it suits her. That said, it is bemusing to me how she can be so worldly on certain things and so hopelessly green on others, but I'll dish more on that later.

Abi is sitting on Fola's left side, chewing on bubblegum like a cow chewing cud on overtime—Abieyuwa Omonitie. Cute and curvy with the smoothest chocolate skin you ever did see, Abi is too friendly, so inquisitive, and she flutters from topic to topic like a parrot with ADD. All of that isn't bad...some of the time.

She is always tuned in to the latest school or celeb gossip and is ever willing to go out of her way to do things for the people she considers important to her. She can be overly sensitive too. Who cried while watching 'The Sound of Music' for heaven's sake? Oh? Let's move on then.

Abi also happens to be one of the most extremely naïve people I know—she's even more so than Fola—which is not such a bad thing either. Fine, I'll cut the crap. Our darling Abi's naiveté and idyllic outlook on life is more surprising when you consider that she is the product of a bitterly broken home.

Her daddy, a now apparently retired wife batterer, has long since remarried and lives with his new family in London. Dear old Daddy forgets more than half of the time that he has an older daughter that he left behind and when he does deign to remember, a paltry box of stale Godiva chocolates suffices.

So dear old Abi is stuck with toxic and bitter old Mommy in a rickety aging two-bedroom apartment on Lagos Island, and bitter old Mommy barely manages to pay the rent working as a teller in a bank in Yaba.

She is mad at men and life in general, so she comes back and takes it all out on poor old Abi who has the batterer's eyes. And while poor old Abi continues to get angrier and angrier at bitter old Mommy, she insists on holding dear old Daddy higher and higher on the pedestal he totally does not deserve. Yes, the worst.

I love Abi to death, but I hate that she is, simply put, too easy and trusting. She tends to take things at face value all the time and that worries me because people who do that, more often than not, learn their lessons too late. I know I did.

Sitting on my right side and gazing absentmindedly into space, like she always gets caught doing, is Bibs. Lebiba Gana is the token silent, reserved and level-headed member of our best friends' club. She is secretly my favorite of the lot.

She is startlingly beautiful in an uncanny way, unquestionably the most gorgeous of us four. Her skin is a gorgeous burnt caramel color tone and she has these dark, piercing eyes that are shadowed by these ridiculously long lashes. They make her look like she's got a lot to hide.

Her father, Alhaji Gana, has three wives and eleven publicly acknowledged children. Wife One, Alhaja Fatima, has four children of her own—twenty-six-year-old Ibrahim, twenty-four-year-old Sani, seventeen-year-old Aminatu and fifteen-year-old Habiba.

Number Two, Hajia Maryam, Lebiba's mother, has eighteen-year-old Lebiba, her younger thirteen-year-old sister, Hauwa and the little three-year-old Abubakar.

Youngest-Wife-Pending-Wife-Number-Four, Hajia Ameera, has thirteen-year-old Asma'u, ten-year-old Habeeb, seven-year-old Muhammad, and the eleven-month-old baby girl, Halima.

For fear of a headache, I must cry off on detailing the long list of the other unofficially acknowledged children. It should be enough to say that their large family house in Victoria Island is crammed full of kids, and maids, and nannies, and tutors, and relatives, and more.

My head pounds at the thought alone but at least, the Gana family has the luxury of being one of those peaceful polygamous families mostly because Al-haji, the patriarch, brooks no nonsense.

Everyone likes Bibs. She smiles. She listens—God, she listens. She rarely gets angry, she is always brokering for peace, and she never, ever has a bad word to say about anyone. Her favorite saying pretty much sums her up—*it's all good*. She says that all the time.

Bibs has always been the hardest one to get through out of my three friends. Secretive and solemn in a way only she can be, you can't help but think that there's much more to her than meets the eye.

And that's the lot of us—Lara, Fola, Abi and Bibs. Four totally different personalities from totally different backgrounds with totally different stories and yet somehow, we make our friendship work.

I like to picture our friendship as a see-saw, you know, with me on one wild, crazy extreme, Bibs, the exact opposite of me on the other end of the conundrum, and we have Fola and Abi in the middle for balance.

Come Monday, we'll begin our second year of Advanced-Level courses (A-Levels, to keep it simple) at Gatesbridge Co-Ed and once the year is up, we will be going our separate ways.

I'm heading to college in America. Bibs and Fola will be heading over to university in England. Abi might stay on here, or perhaps her father will grow some balls, defy his new wife, and ask her to come over and join his new family in London. Miracles do happen.

Despite the impending separation, we've sworn to be friends for life, which is all nice and dandy but given that I tend to overdose on reality, a rather depressing belief strikes me every now and then—time moves on, so do people.

My mom barely remembers her chief bridesmaid, never mind the name of her best friend in college, and I seem to emulate all the shit she does. You know, like lying. Like lying daddy dearest right into a non-existent grave before resur-recting him like he was Lazarus.

My, I've done an excellent job of coming across as quite the jaded individual but hey, we're all jaded, albeit some more than others, no? We only differ in expressing how jaded we are. Some, like me, act out. Others like Fola and Abi live like they wouldn't even recognize the word if it were flashed before them in bold scarlet letters. Still others, like Lebiba, hide it.

So, there we have it. There ends what was supposed to be the mundane in-troduction to this story—a story which, as I have explained, was going to be a perfectly ordinary yet prettily embroidered tale about the four of us before life went ahead to do what it does best.

You know the one about throwing a curveball and all? Yes, it did that and then some.

CHAPTER TWO

Fola

FIRST DAY OF SCHOOL. Check.

Clean monogrammed towel. Check.

Ironed uniform. Check. Polished shoes. Check.

Steaming mug of tea. Check.

The maid had not missed a beat today and everything was in order, thankfully. I had to rip her a new you-know-what yesterday evening for not having my dinner ready on time.

On a regular school morning, it would take me roughly an hour to get ready but given that I had gotten up later than usual this morning, Mommy was already calling me out from the dining room by the time I hopped out of the shower and into my school uniform.

"Yes, Mommy!" I yelled as I flew down the stairs.

"Be careful!" She raised her eyebrows as I came stumbling into the dining room. Gee, you would think everything in the dining room was made of glass or marble. Wait, almost everything was.

Mommy was already dressed for work in what I liked to call her black power suit. A consultant for the Lagos State Government, she had a flexible schedule that allowed her to set her hours and travel as she pleased. She also sold jewelry from Dubai—a lucrative venture—in her spare time. Daddy made enough so that she didn't have to work but she loved to keep herself busy.

I slid into my seat as two maids brought out table settings for me and Sayo, my younger and only brother.

"What do you want to eat?" One of the maids asked.

"Toast, please," I answered.

"I want toast," Sayo said, "and I want that with pancakes and corned beef stew too."

"How is that potbelly you're grooming?" I had to ask.

"Mind your business!" He snapped.

The cheek of the boy. Only fourteen and we were already bearing the brunt of his puberty woes.

"You mind how you talk to me!" I retorted.

Mommy moved to defuse the brewing argument. "Not this morning, the two of you. It's too early for all that."

Daddy showed up then, attempting to adjust his tie and read the morning paper at the same time.

"Good morning, sir," Sayo and I said together.

He grunted in reply, picked up his briefcase from the bottom of the stairway and waving distractedly, he shot out of the door.

"The COMMUNET deal closes today," Mommy said ruefully as she gingerly buttered a slice of bread.

I rolled my eyes. I did not understand why she insisted on making excuses for him. It was the same old scene every morning—Daddy rushing out the door before any one of us could set our eyes on him.

The consummate workaholic, he was often away for weeks, months, at a stretch and we were used to it. The unspoken truth around here was the money was expected to make up for his absence. I loved my daddy—he could be a fun-loving, boisterous and generous man...when he had the time—but to put it nicely, as long as I got what I wanted when I needed it, I could have seen him less than once in a year and it would suit me just fine.

Mommy and Sayo were having a conversation over my head as I made myself a sandwich with the warm, toasted bread, margarine, and Cook's sunnyside-up eggs. Lara's running joke was that breakfast at ours was akin to having the continental breakfast at a five-star hotel, you know, with cereals, pastries, fruits, tea, coffee, milk and juices, the works.

I tuned into the conversation in time to hear Mommy say, "Sayo, Mr. Adelola will start lessons with you today at five o'clock so make sure you're ready for him."

"I don't need lessons!" He cried loudly.

Yeah, right.

"Let Mr. Adelola be the judge of that. We were not too pleased with your grades last term."

"I'll do better this term on my own!"

"Your father and I will rather not risk that."

"Why are we acting like Daddy looked at my report card? You know he didn't!"

Mommy bit her next words out. "Watch that tongue, young man! Your lessons start at five o'clock today and that is that!"

I stifled my chuckle as the truant got put in his place for once.

Shortly afterwards, we were heading for school in the white Lexus SUV with Sayo still grumbling in the backseat, of course.

Lara was already in the classroom at her desk when I walked in.

"Hey, early bird!" I flopped down in the seat next to hers. "You were that eager to come back to school?"

She turned around to roll her eyes at me. "I wish! You should have heard me cursing when my alarm went off this morning. Just as well this is the last year of this school stuff."

My archenemy passed by as I opened my mouth to respond. Bisola. She always had it out for me for some inexplicable reason. The dislike had become very, very mutual and I never missed an opportunity to make that clear to her on my part.

"Complaining as usual, huh?" She jeered as she marched past my desk.

Someone decidedly wanted me to draw blood this morning and I was more than up to it.

"Hey, hey, hey! Excuse me, was I by any chance talking to you?" I asked in a dismissive tone.

She rose to the bait as usual. "I see you haven't realized that the sound of your voice is an irritant to the majority of mankind."

"And clearly, you're yet to realize that you will never be fortunate enough to be a part of the smarter and more privileged minority."

"All hail Miss Richie-Rich!" She snorted.

I went in for the kill. "Hey, don't blame me because your father can hardly afford to pay school fees for you and—what was the number at the last count—fifteen siblings? Girl, bye!"

I heard muted *oooooohs* in the background from the rest of our classmates.

"Fola, don't you dare talk about my father!"

"Then you, my friend, don't go buying trouble you can't afford because you know me, I'll give it to you for free!"

More muted *ooooooohs*. Our heated argument was fast becoming a spectacle that I was only too willing to keep up had Bibs, the peacemaker, not shown up then.

"Come on, you guys. Are you serious? On the first day of school?" she asked in her soft, placating voice.

"You'd better tell this idiot to get out of my face then!" I kissed my teeth.

"I don't blame you!" Bisola spat at me before storming off.

Our audience melted away begrudgingly as she did so.

"Fola!" Bibs shook her head as she took her place in front of Lara and me.

I rolled my eyes and glanced at Lara who was curled over in hysterical laughter. "You didn't call out her father and his wandering cockatoo, you cow!"

From the corner of my eye, I saw Bibs purse her lips. She hated it when Lara got crass. You would think she'd get used to it already.

"She'll think twice before crossing my lane next time," I said grimly.

"It's all good. Where's Abi? Late as usual?" Bibs asked in an obvious attempt to change the subject.

"You don't worry," Lara said, "you know her. She'll make it here at the exact second the bell goes off for assembly."

"I hope her mother isn't giving her trouble as usual."

Classic Bibs for you, our resident Mother Theresa. She was always out to carry everyone else's troubles on her head. '*Igba onigba*', like Mommy would say.

Speaking of mothers, Abi had a witch for one. She was justifiably bitter and scorned—her husband did leave her for another woman after years of using, or rather, abusing her as his punching bag. However, why she unleashed her rage on Abi was anybody's guess. I did not understand how Abi remained sane. Better death than that, in my humble opinion.

Thinking about it, I was just about the sole one out of the gang with a standard, regular family.

Lara's parents had divorced when she was a toddler, and she had not known about her dad and two older brothers until she had moved back to Nigeria at fourteen. Crazy!

There was Bibs with her stepmothers and way too many half-siblings. There was no hostile rivalry and all that jazz in her home but that was because her daddy was super strict and repressive.

He had so many ridiculous rules—Bibs and her sisters were not allowed to wear pants (skirts were the order of the day and had to be a certain length, including their school uniforms), or stay out after an evening curfew that started at nine, or go to some places without a chaperone—and they were all afraid to get into his black book because he had an exceedingly black temper. Crazy.

Abi had a witch for a mother and a wannabe boxer (who was in denial he has a daughter called Abi) for a father. Crazy.

So yes, I considered myself the only one with a regular family. I loved my best friends but gee, was I thankful I was not them!

A warning bell tolled and there was a rising crescendo of noise as I, along with everyone else (Abi was so late!), hastily jumped up and made our way downstairs to the assembly hall for the morning prayers and rituals.

CHAPTER THREE

Abi

I COULDN'T RISK A QUICK glance at the mirror because Mumsie was already shouting for me.

"Abieyuwa!" She screeched. "Why are you bent on wasting my time this morning? I will leave you behind *o*, you this girl!"

Jeez, could she at least let me grab breakfast first? Grimacing, I hastily stuffed a piece of bread slathered with Blue-Band margarine into my mouth and ran out speedily where my mother was waiting in her old, white Honda.

I slid into the car, chewing. We made the drive to school in dead silence because as usual, Mumsie and I rarely had much to say to each other except for when we were exchanging harsh words.

Mumsie had a personal vendetta against me for not being the son my father wanted. Like it was my fault. I wanted badly to pack up and go live with Popsie in London, but his new wife was having yet another baby, and they had no more room, and blah, blah, blah. Long story short, I was stuck here with the shrew. For now.

Assembly was wrapping up when I arrived at school, but I was lucky enough to sneak up to class without being seen. Within minutes, everyone began streaming into the classroom from the assembly hall, my friends included.

"Latecomer!" Fola playfully pushed at my head as she walked past me to her desk.

"How did the patrol miss you?" Bibs wanted to know. She was referring to the teachers who stalked the hallways during assembly so they could swoop down on any unsuspecting student who was late or playing truant.

I grinned. "I slipped in through the stairs at the back!"

"Bad!" Lara wagged her head at me.

I smiled again. I didn't know where I would be without these three girls. They made life bearable for me, especially when the going got rough at home.

"What have we got this morning?" I asked, trying but failing to stifle a yawn.

"A double period of Economics, another double period of Math," the ever-ready Bibs recited, "then, a single period of Chemistry slash Accounting, all of that before break time."

"Economics, noooo!" Lara groaned loudly. We all made gagging sounds at the thought of Economics, one of our least favorite subjects taught by our least favorite teacher.

Ms. Odulami, our class teacher, looked up from her table where she was taking attendance.

"Mayowa, get off that table! And you, take that gum out of your mouth right now, my friend!" She snapped at Fola, who made a face and tossed out the stale gum she had been chewing.

I rummaged through my backpack, laughing. My laughter trailed away as I realized I did not have my Economics textbook on me.

"Jeez, I forgot my Econ textbook!"

"Who wouldn't?" Lara laughed.

"It's not funny. You have yours on you!"

"Are you sure you own one?" That was Bibs.

"Focus, guys! I don't want to be sent out of class and on the first day too! Princi might see me!" Princi was the moniker for our strict principal, Mr. Neil Sasegbon.

"It's only an hour or so. You won't miss much so what's the big deal?" Fola chipped in.

"Okay for you to say. You have your book on you too!" I said to her. "Miss a whole two-period class on our first day back? Come off it!"

"Doesn't Emeka have an extra textbook? You should borrow it off him before someone else does." Bibs suggested.

I shuddered. Emeka was one of the class nerds and he did not exactly have sanitary habits.

"God forbid!" I exaggeratedly snapped my fingers over my head. "I'll rather be kicked out of class!"

Lara laughed. "Huh! You must secretly want to miss this class!"

The noise level escalated as Ms. Odulami left the classroom and then died an abrupt death the second our Economics teacher, Mr. Iyiola, walked in. The man was a complete prick who ruled his classes with an iron hand.

"Good morning, class!" He shouted in his too-loud, booming voice.

"Good morning, sir!" The class responded.

Moving towards the blackboard, he shouted again. "Absent notes, absent textbooks, uncompleted notes and so on and so forth…if you fall under any of these categories, please leave my class!"

I quickly motioned to Emeka. My friends stifled their giggles and I flashed them indignant looks as I stretched to collect his spare textbook. Today was not designed to be my lucky day, however, because Mr. Iyiola's wandering eye fell on Emeka as he passed the book over to me.

"Abieyuwa Omonitie and Emeka Obiakor. What is the matter?"

"Nothing, sir!" We both chorused.

"Nothing?"

Shoot.

He skulked over to my seat and in seconds, he was towering over me forbiddingly.

"Nothing, you say?"

"No, sir!" I whimpered. "I-I-I was collecting the book that I lent Emeka last term."

"Is that so?" Mr. Iyiola picked up the offending textbook. "Because if that is so, Emeka must be a thief-in-waiting or why else would his name be written on your textbook?"

The overzealous Emeka, in an effort to clear his name, cried out. "Ah! Excuse me, sir, it's my textbook! I borrowed her this morning!"

I turned and eyed him. If looks could kill, he would have been roasted to a crisp and buried as far down underground as he could go.

"So, Abi is the liar-in-waiting and you both are criminals-in-waiting. No room for criminals in my class! I'm sure you know what I mean." Mr. Iyiola smirked.

"But sir—" I began, ready to protest.

"Five hundred lines, tomorrow morning at 8 o'clock prompt, 'I must not lie to Mr. Iyiola'. I don't want to have to remind you. Now, leave my class. I have leaders of tomorrow to attend to."

I hissed and picking up my books, I made to walk out of the classroom, Emeka following close behind.

"Abieyuwa, make that a thousand lines until you learn to control that hissing noise that makes you sound like an insipid snake!" Mr. Iyiola barked.

I rushed out of class before my rebellious tongue could betray me again. I barely restrained myself from ripping apart the excuse of a textbook in my hand, flinging it angrily instead at its irritating owner. The stupid book had palm oil smeared all over it and smelled like fruit gone bad.

I had to skip all my classes before the break period to finish my lines because I would not have the time to do them at home, not with the zillion chores to get done.

By the time the break rolled around, and my friends joined me at our usual spot—the concrete ledge under the gum tree—I was in a rather cranky mood.

"You skipped all your classes, Abi!" Fola dropped down beside me on the ledge.

"I had to finish the stupid lines," I replied sulkily.

"Were you at least able to get it all done?" Lara asked.

"Most of it. I should be done before the end of the day."

There was a lull in our conversation as we dug into the sausage rolls Lara picked up from the tuck shop and then, Fola turned to Bibs. "So, did you get around to asking your dad if you could come out Saturday night?"

We were planning on going as a crew to a house party in Ikoyi this weekend (someone almost always threw a party the first weekend of every new school term) but Bibs was having trouble getting permission from her father as usual. I was luckier. All I had to do was tell Mumsie that I was staying over at Fola's and she would be cool. She liked Fola, my 'rich friend'.

"I don't think I am going to bother. He's going to say the same thing he always says, which is an 'N' and an 'O'!" Bibs answered.

"How will you know if you don't try?" Fola asked again.

"I'd like to think I know my father better than you do," Bibs told her crossly.

"Well, if he is being as stuffy as always and still won't let you have some fun, we'll go without you then!"

Fola could be a brat sometimes.

"You know, Fola, sometimes you can be so selfish," Lara said, voicing my thoughts. "It's not like she's the only one who's got a father who isn't shit. Yours isn't, either!"

Ouch. Bibs and I winced visibly.

Classic Lara for you. She had mastered the fine art of making hurtful and caustic remarks in the most pleasant and laid-back voice, and the remarks never failed to hit their target because they were the plain and bitter truth. Even worse, she didn't see or more like, didn't care about the hurt she inflicted on people that way. It was one of the more dangerous things about her, in my opinion.

Fola glared at her in outrage. "That's my daddy you're talking about!"

Lara snorted lazily. "You didn't have a problem talking about Bibs' dad just now!"

Bibs cut in mildly. "There's no need to argue over this. I'll ask my father but if he says no, you guys can go ahead without me. It's all good."

"As if!" Lara grinned impishly. "If he says no, we'll all hang out instead. I'm sure your father will let you out, at least for that!"

Bibs stuck out her tongue at her and smiled.

Seeing Fola still sulking, Lara leaned over and grabbed her into a bear hug.

"You know I love you, my darling!" She cooed, trying to kiss Fola's cheeks which made the reluctant recipient of the kisses smile begrudgingly. "I love all of you! I can't believe this will be our last year together!"

"Don't remind us." I sighed heavily.

Finally managing to push Lara off her, Fola said, "It might be our last year together but that doesn't change a thing because we'll always be friends. I mean, look at us, there's nothing we don't know about each other, nothing we don't share with each other. Wherever we end up after this isn't going to change that. Our friendship is forever, guys, forever!"

"Forever!" The rest of us hooted, catching on to her enthusiasm.

The dynamics of a four-way friendship could be, for lack of a better word, interesting, and mostly because our different relationships with each other were unique. Lara and Bibs got along best, which made sense considering they were extreme opposites. Bibs had the softer personality that rubbed away Lara's rough edges, and Lara had the louder personality that drew Bibs out.

She would never admit it, but everyone knew Fola resented Bibs' relationship with Lara because she (Fola) was particularly drawn to Lara, one of the few people who refused to submit to her sometimes excessive and domineering personality.

I flippantly called myself the 'make-do' friend because Fola used me to fill the gap she wished Lara would. And despite my knowing that, Fola remained the first person I would turn to if I needed anything.

Lara frightened me and we were the least close duo out of the crew. And Bibs was Bibs. She got along with everybody and I was no exception. She was just...a little too perfect for me.

All that to say, our friendship required an intricate balance which could be easily upset by little disagreements like the scene now between Fola and Bibs but fortunately, we had discovered when it came to our friendship, the sum of the whole was greater than its parts.

And you know, because of that, Fola was right. Our friendship was going to be forever. Forever ever.

CHAPTER FOUR
Bibs

...BYE, SEPTEMBER. IT has been relatively quiet since the school term began, mostly because Alhaji was away for a good part of the month.

What would life be if we did not have to look over our shoulders for him? That is one castle in the air that will never be built. See you in October.

EXHALING LOUDLY, I remove my reading glasses and drop the book Lara lent me. I manage to rouse my lazy self from the beanbag I have been reclining on to amble over to my dressing table.

Staring blankly at my reflection, I unravel the braid I had bound my hair into and begin to brush it dispassionately. The brushing has become a ritual of sorts for me when I need to escape a crowded mind.

I inherited my mother's curly rope of hair which I am sometimes tempted to snip off because the braid I am forced to always keep it in has come to represent a sign of oppression to me.

Even my clothes reek of oppression. At the moment, I'm wearing a brown plaid blouse and a pleated skirt. Can you say oppressively boring? I don't know that I have ever owned a pair of denim pants or casual slacks.

Girls in trousers, Alhaji would never have that. He practically designs and decides the clothes that we wear, and he does not stop there either, you see. He runs our lives, lives it for us. The man is nothing if not thorough.

I hate him. No, I don't. I'm not sure.

I am still brushing away compulsively. The curls in my hair get tangled easily when they are fresh out of a braid. I have never gotten a perm. One of my sisters risked asking once and Alhaji had smacked her across the face.

Such vanity in a devotee of God, he had said, his cold voice dripping with disgust. We all know not to ever ask again. She has a scar now that reminds us never to forget in case we do.

I am still brushing. One day, I will brush all my hair right off my head.

Devotee of God. I snort. He has called me more sordid names. Could I count them all? No, but it's all good.

I startle, losing my train of thought as my three-year old brother, Abu totters into the room, whimpering.

"Leba!" He held up his arms as he waddled over to me. He has not yet learned to pronounce my name correctly, you see.

My throat tightens as I pick him up and put him on my lap. I inhale the comforting scent of baby powder and ask, "What's wrong?"

"Muhammad hit me," he says forlornly in Hausa.

"English, Abu!" I reprimand him gently. "Always in English, I keep telling you."

Muhammad, the venerable bully, comes in then.

"What did you do to Abu, Muhammad?" I ask the seven-year old tyrant.

"What did you do to Abu?" He repeats in Hausa, knowing it would annoy me.

"Answer me!"

"He's stupid! He woke Halima up and Nurse blamed me!"

"He's your brother. Don't call him stupid!"

"He's not my brother! Habeeb says he's a bastard!"

That renders me speechless, not the word itself but more Habeeb's obvious malice in saying so to Muhammad. I make a mental note to deal with him later.

Struggling for composure, I scold Muhammad while twisting his ear. "If I ever hear that word from your mouth again, I'll knock your head so hard that you'll be seeing stars for one week! You hear me?"

Nodding soberly and almost in tears, he slinks out of the room.

Abu is tugging at my skirt now. I push Muhammad's words from my mind with difficulty. "What now, baba?"

"Hungry," he says in his baby English, pointing to his mouth.

I smile at his attempt. "Will you have rice?"

He nods keenly so I take him downstairs to the kitchen where I dish out steamed rice and curry sauce for him in his favorite Sesame Street bowl. As I fix him a cup of blackcurrant juice and set him on his chair to eat, my mother's younger daughter, Hauwa, comes in, complaining of a stomach-ache.

"Have you eaten?" She is prone to theatrics, my little sister.

"I'm not hungry," she moans. "It bites and my back aches all over. It's so uncomfortable."

Amina, my stepmother's daughter, joins us then. Amina is the sibling I am closest to, which is mainly because she is the closest in age to me out of my father's children, and we share a room.

"What's wrong?" She asks Hauwa. After listening to some whining, she adds, "don't worry. Go and lie down upstairs. We'll bring Advil and hot tea for you so you feel better, hmm?"

"What could be wrong with her?" Amina turns to me as Hauwa goes upstairs and she prepares to make the hot tea.

"Who knows? Maybe she ate something off."

"I did think that casserole last night tasted a bit funny." She smirks.

"Amina, you always think everything tastes funny. Just admit it, you hate the cook," I say, my eyes on Abu. "Don't spill your rice, baba. Put the spoon—"

A loud, ungodly shriek from upstairs cuts short my little lecture.

My heart in my throat, I race upstairs with Amina hot on my heels. We both stumble into the room Hauwa shares with our two other half-sisters, Habiba and Asma'u, and into the bathroom where Hauwa is, wailing.

"Hauwa, what happened? What's wrong?" I ask loudly, trying to cut through her hysterics.

"I'm bleeding!"

"Bleeding? Where? What happened? Did you cut yourself?"

"I don't know...it's on my underwear!" she cries. "I came to use the bathroom and saw it! It's everywhere!"

She starts wailing again.

I heave a sigh of relief and shake my head at my clueless sister. In a frenzy over her first period – Hajia has evidently never had the conversation with her. No surprises there.

I signal to her to wait and head for my room to fetch some sanitary towels.

"What's wrong with her?" Amina asks anxiously as I walk out of the bathroom.

"Don't mind her. I have no idea what they're teaching them in Biology classes these days."

It takes some time to settle Hauwa down, and it is only after she is cleaned up and lying comfortably in bed with a mug of herbal tea, that I let out a snort of bottled-up laughter.

"You're such a drama queen! Did you have to make such a scene?"

She flushes. "I was scared! I didn't know what was happening!"

"Now, you do and it's nothing to be scared of. It just means you're not such a baby anymore. You know what could happen now, don't you?"

"Yes," she replies. "I've heard that...you can get pregnant if you...mess around."

At least that she knows.

"And I'm sure you already know Alhaji will not have that at all," I say awkwardly, not knowing what else to say. I am certainly not the best person to have this conversation about the birds and the bees with.

"I know that. I hate it, Lebiba! It feels so weird and disgusting. Why me?"

I smile. "It's not just you, Hauwa. We all go through it too."

"But it hurts!"

"Don't worry, the pills will help. You can think of it as a sacrifice you need to make if you want to have babies in the future at the right time."

"Lebiba, is this...like what you went through?" she asks me, bug-eyed. "You know...that time?"

I eye her speculatively. "Um, something like it but let's not talk about that now."

"I'm sorry," she hurriedly says before sighing. "Lebiba, it really hurts."

I nod. "I know, dear. The pills will kick in, don't worry."

We lean against each other while I rub her back before I think to ask, "So Hajia never spoke to you about any of this?"

"You know Hajia now."

They do not make them any more in denial than our mother, you see.

"It's all good," I tell Hauwa. "I'll let her know about this so she can speak to you, but you do have some common sense of your own and you won't go getting into trouble, right?"

Hauwa smiles. "You should be my mother."

I smile back at her sadly.

Back in my room, I make my way to my bathroom, making sure to lock the door before I sink to the floor. Hauwa's initial fit has terrified me much more than I thought. The fear is only now creeping in. Her loud screams were so reminiscent of the time when...

No, I mustn't think about that. I mustn't! I tell myself fiercely.

The self-admonition does not have the desired effect. Already, I have to shove my fist in my mouth to choke back the racking sobs before Amina walks in and hears me.

The innocence in Hauwa's eyes is a ticking bomb. It will not be long now before it fades from her eyes. Then she will stare at me with eyes as empty as mine, silently accusing me for not warning her about the path to come...the path that others, including me, have already traveled.

It's not fair. It's not fair. It's not fair. I whisper to myself as the scenes replay in my head like a horror movie directed by the devil himself. Location of scene – pits of hell...*jahannam.*

Almost blinded by tears, I reach up for the razor blade secured in its usual spot—tucked away in the gap between the ceramic sink and the concrete wall. I lift my skirt and brace myself. Funny, no matter how hard I brace myself, I am never fully ready for that first slice of pain.

Lowering my hand, I strike at the pale flesh underneath my skirt again, and again, and again, and again, and again until my movements are almost a blur in front of my eyes. The pain is bittersweet as it flows through me, and the blood is a dull red as it flows out of me.

As always, it is a relief, if just for a while, to escape the harsh reality that surrounds me. It is a relief to have the focus of my world intensely narrowed to the twinges of my open wounds.

Yes, it was real. Yes, it had happened.

Once again, I am vindicated. I pant heavily, tears running down my cheeks, as I scrutinize the cuts, both old and new, and the fresh blood coagulating on the discolored bathroom floor tiles.

CHAPTER FIVE

Lara

...WE'VE BEEN AT MOM'S an extra week because Dad had to travel to Lisbon for work. The shuffling between houses never gets old! Imagine a world where I never got the chance to meet my dad, Mayode, and Modupe, a world where Mom never left James, where Mom and I never left Virginia and moved to Lagos...

I can't help pondering on this...and the things we left behind.

I SNUFFED OUT MY CIGARETTE and smiled guiltily as Modupe, my second older brother, joined me on the balcony I had stolen out to earlier. I pushed the pack of Marlboro Lights into my back pocket as he approached.

"Lara!" His tone was gentle yet reproachful.

"Hey, big brother, and I mean that literally!"

He laughed. "The Federal Ministry of Health warns that..."

"...tobacco smoking is dangerous to health!" I finished. I winked at him and we both cracked up.

"On a serious note..." He started again.

"Come on now, I'm trying! It used to be five sticks a day!"

"A stick a day does more than enough damage." He motioned for me to hand him the pack. Rats.

I had loads of bad habits. Smoking was one of the worst and it'd been a headache trying to kick the habit which I stupidly picked up for a laugh when I was twelve. Yeah, twelve, sue me. My darling brother, Modupe, had been the most aggressive in trying to get me to quit.

It was in truth a surreal experience getting to know the two brothers I never knew existed until I was fourteen. Courtesy of Julius—Dad, I mean—Mayode and Modupe at least knew that they had a runaway mother and a tag-along sister somewhere out there. I had been the sole blindsided clown.

What was the inside story? Quick recap—Portugal met Nigeria. Portugal and Nigeria fell in love and got married. A couple years and three kids later, Portugal and Nigeria realized that things were no longer working out for them.

Mom, recovering from postpartum depression at the time (having just had me), had rashly filed for a divorce and left Portugal for America (literally, this time), taking four-month old me along with her.

She would have taken the boys along, but my dad had stood his ground—his boys were going nowhere. To date, I didn't get that part. His boys had been worth fighting for but not me? Huh.

Mom had remarried and become Mrs. James Wilder a year after she moved to America and for fourteen years, I had grown up oblivious of the rest of my family in Portugal at the time. Mom had told me some ambiguous story of my dad dying before I was born and so James, my stepfather, had been the father figure for me during my formative years.

Mom and James had divorced when I turned thirteen and a year after that, I had become too much trouble for my mom, triggering her decision to move back to Lagos.

Again, she had not expected to run into the ex-husband she had left behind in Portugal. Said ex-husband had moved to Nigeria to manage the new subsidiary of a construction company headquartered in Portugal.

To cut the shitty tale short, I spent the years since that fortuitous meeting getting to know my dad and my two brothers.

My dad took up my tuition and living costs, enrolled me in school with my brothers, and picked up the buck to my mom's relief.

Under my dad's dutiful hand, I apparently became more of the daughter my mom wanted me to be. In her opinion, anyway. Now, we were all living happily after, right?

Okay, obviously, things did not straighten out so smoothly. For starters, I was terribly angry at my mother for a long time. I still was. She was not a bad mother per se, but she had not been the world's best mom either. Yes, she had stepped up and demanded a divorce from the charming, manipulative Mr. Wilder but she could have done that much earlier.

Then she had had the nerve to lie to me about my father and my brothers. It blew my mind to date how she was able to tell such a lie to a child. All the time I'd felt alone, she had known and never breathed a word. For crying out loud, she had her stupid James. I had nobody! I had nobody but sure, bygones were bygones.

And there was my dad, so eager to make up for the lost time. What the fuck e-v-e-r. Where the hell had he been he all that time? How could he have let my mother leave with me? How could he have so easily agreed to let my brothers and I be separated that long?

He had not cared enough to reach out and find out about his daughter as the years went by. If Fate had not played our family like its favorite fiddle, I would have lived out the rest of my life not knowing he and my brothers existed. He had let some flipping stranger try to be the father that he was meant to be. Newsflash, Dad. That stranger failed. That stranger failed big time but sure, bygones were bygones.

Neither my dad nor my mom was aware of the resentment I held towards them. I loved them, yes, but a part of me would always hate them because they could have done a whole lot better. They had one job, one, but meh, I had never been too fond of the principle of parents anyway.

Besides, I had my brothers who I had come to love to death. Mayode was my oldest brother. He was twenty-one and a Business major at NYU. Modupe was exactly a year and a half older than I was—nineteen years and some change. He finished his A-Levels last year but decided to take a gap year to kick off his music career before heading to college next year.

Spending alternate weeks between our parents meant that we did an awful lot of shuttling between my mom's duplex in Lekki and my dad's townhouse in Ikoyi. That had taken some getting used to, along with the fact that I now had to share my mom with my brothers.

She had to learn to divide her attention among three children and it seemed to me, at first, that she was spending extra time and care on them to make up for her abandonment (my brothers would probably say they felt the same way about Dad and me).

So yeah, my brothers and I have had to work through some major issues. Unlike me, they seemed to be over it but see, Dad never remarried. Mom had.

"Hello, guys!" The woman in question smiled as Modupe and I walked into the kitchen together in search of food.

"I'm hungry," I said, heading straight for the fridge. Modupe threw his arms around her waist, nearly folding her in half with his six-feet-two frame.

"Modupe! *O mo pe o ti n d'agba*?" She laughed as he resisted her attempts to throw him off so she could breathe. I rolled my eyes at the fact that my brother needed reminding that he was growing way too old for antics like jumping on his mama.

"What do you want to eat?" I heard her ask as I peeked in the refrigerator.

"No clue. What do you have to offer?"

"There's fried rice and salad, and there are meat pies in the microwave. I have to leave now. I'm meeting with a customer at six."

She was an interior decorator here in Lagos and, I was proud to see, an increasingly popular one.

"I want pounded yam!" Modupe whined.

"Ah, that will have to wait until I get back! I have to go now! By the way, Mayode called earlier for you guys but you weren't home yet. He's going to call back later."

"We'll Skype him," I told her.

"Good. I'll see you kids later."

"Bye, Mom!" Modupe cried from the den where he was already digging into a hastily microwaved meat pie.

"Call Mayode," he said with his mouth full when I joined him.

"I will if you'll turn down the TV."

We got through to Mayode after struggling with the crappy network. Shortly after the ensuing boisterous conversation was over, the landline (yes, Mom was quaint like that) rang. I picked it up at the double.

"Dara, is that you?" It was my dad. He was in Lisbon, a business trip he made often.

"Hey! Nope, this is Lara. Mom's out."

"Where is she? I've been trying to reach her on her cell."

"She just stepped out of the house. She had to meet up with a customer or something."

He left a message for my mom and asked about Modupe and school before he rang off. Seconds after I dropped the landline, my mobile phone rang. *Sheesh!*

"Hello."

"Hey, babe!"

"It could have been my mom who picked up, you know."

He scoffed at that. "Yeah, because I'm such an idiot and I can't tell the difference between your voices."

He was Manny Harriman, Manny being short for Amananaowei, the Izon word for king. Manny was from central Ijaw and had lived in over five different countries, thanks to his father who became an ambassador before he was born. He had vivid memories of their sojourns. His mother died when he was five, so he did not remember as much about her.

He was his mother's only child and his father never remarried. What his father did do was accumulate a long line of mistresses and ensuing kids, the time he had for each decreasing accordingly. All told, the circumstances had resulted in Manny growing up to be an über spoilt and wild brat with no regard for authority and societal norm. Did I mention he was my boyfriend? Yeah, my kinda guy.

"You're such a brat!" I knew he could hear the smile in my voice.

"I'm on your side of town."

"So what?"

"Be there in fifteen." He cut the call abruptly. No manners or tact whatsoever.

My mom could not stand him. "He's twenty and has no idea what he wants to do with his life?" she asked me one time, aghast. What did she know anyway? She married James, for chrissake. Manny, or Amana as I preferred to call him, was not the conventional type, never had been, and likely never would be

"And that bike?" My mom went on.

Manny rode a motorbike to the horror of a lot of people. Even I, as extremely open-minded as I was, experienced a sense of trepidation when it came to Manny's bike. It was not the bike, per se. It was more of Manny on the bike. I called that bike Satan to his utter annoyance because that was his baby...after me, of course.

Manny made it to my mom's house in five. He was waiting in the formal living room when I walked in.

"Amana!" He absolutely hated when I called him that.

He eyed me coolly and beckoned at me to come closer.

I squeezed onto his lap and gave him a quick kiss.

"Want to go for a spin on the bike?" He asked each time he came over.

My reply was always the same. "Never!"

"How about a smoke then?"

"I've had my quota for today. You should be encouraging me to quit!" I smacked him lightly.

He snorted. "Right."

"What's going on? Did you get up to anything today?" I asked.

"Nah, I do have some news for you, though. Guess who got their admission letter from the University of Texas?" he said off-handedly.

Manny recently applied to study Petroleum Engineering in his quest to make a difference to the despicable condition of the Niger Delta—he claimed he did so out of his passion for the oil-rich but piss-poor region of our country but really, he wanted his share of the oil dollars. I'd been dreading his potential move in January, less than four months away, but I was so excited now to hear he got accepted to the college of his choice.

"What? No way! No, you did not! Wait, you're just telling me? When did you find out?"

"Calm down, I got the heads-up today. It was actually mailed to my aunt who called my old man."

I gave him a big, fat smack on his lips. "My goodness, my very own Petroleum minister! I'm proud of you! And they thought you couldn't do it! What did your dad say?"

"He's over the moon!" He grinned. "I'm giving him at least one reason to claim me at last. He's been crowing all day, talking about having a celebration dinner this weekend."

I laughed and kissed him again. "I'm so flipping proud of you! So, you're going to go for sure?"

"Eh, I've had enough of being a bum. I might as well try something different. I could always drop out if I'm not into it."

"You're silly!"

"Tell me about it. What do you say we go off and have our own little cele-bration?"

"What did you have in mind?"

"My room, my bed." He smirked.

"You're an idiot."

"We could go for dinner, but we'll end up in my room at the end of the day so why not cut to the chase?"

"Do you ever think of anything else?"

"Is that a yes?" He ruffled my hair.

"We're not going on your bike."

"I love you."

"No, we're not!"

"Whatever, killjoy. Come, let's make out."

I smacked his head and squealed as he tickled me in retaliation.

"I'm going to miss you like hell when I leave," he whispered.

My mood changed instantly. "Can we not talk about that right now, babe?"

"Tell me you love me then."

Stupid, needy boy.

"I love you."

There was nothing like being needed.

CHAPTER SIX

Abi

...AND I HADN'T HEARD from Popsie in a minute so I cajoled Lara into getting me call credit so I could call him yesterday. He sounded happy to hear from me, I think. We couldn't talk for too long as he was running late for a meeting.

I did remind him to send university brochures and he promised he would. Take that, Mumsie! She laughs mockingly whenever I remind her that he has agreed for me to come live with him in England after my A-Levels. She hates on him for no reason. No wonder he left.

I GROANED LOUDLY. I'D forgotten to wash the pile of clothes Mumsie handed to me this morning and now, it was too late to do so. She was already tooting her car horn loudly at the gate.

Crap!

I dropped my head in my hands and waited for the inevitable storm. God bestowed Mumsie with a noticeably short leash on her temper and more frequently than not, she got bent out of shape over the stupidest things.

I squared up for battle as the door to the small two-bedroom flat we both lived in swung open forcefully. In she came followed by the sickly-sweet scent of her counterfeit perfume.

I murmured something that sounded like a greeting but was not.

She murmured something in return that sounded like a reply but was not.

I watched, irritated, as she dropped her bag on the small dining table in a corner of the living room and sat down heavily on a chair to remove her uncomfortable, too-small office shoes.

"Abi," she eventually said, "bring me some cold water to drink. Then you'll bring out the chicken stew from the freezer. Do we have plantain in the house?"

I shrugged and went into the kitchen—the size of a cupboard, I swear to God—to do as she asked.

When I returned with the water, she snapped at me. "You didn't answer my question."

"There is no plantain," I told her brusquely, barely restraining myself from hissing at her. I settled for pursing my lips instead.

"Is that why you couldn't answer me the first time I asked, *ehn*?"

I ignored her.

"This water is not cold now!" She complained after taking a sip.

"There's been no light since we left this morning."

"Ah, NEPA!" She kissed her teeth, like calling out the old moniker of the rebranded electricity industry that never failed to *not* provide power despite the high bills they demanded, would do the trick.

"Anyway, have you done your homework?" she asked as she rubbed her cramped feet.

I shrugged. Since when did she care about my homework?

"My friend, will you answer me when I ask you a question?"

I rewarded her with sealed lips.

"I don't blame you. One day, I will twist off that your mouth since you don't know how to use it."

I held back from putting my hands to my ears to block out her grating voice. Days like this, I wished Popsie would hurry and send for me to live with him in London. I tried instead to focus on my Accounting homework which was due tomorrow.

The sound of the day's Punch newspaper rustled in the air as Mumsie used it as a makeshift fan, trying to cool off in the searing humid heat of the night. She claimed she had no money to spend on a generator and so, we were stuck with an anemic power inverter that could not sustain the air conditioning, talk less of a standing fan.

"Abi, what about those clothes I asked you to wash?" My mother inevitably asked after polishing off her dinner and making me clear away the plates.

I pretended not to have heard her.

"Abi," she said again, "did you not hear me? I didn't see the clothes drying on the line outside. Where are they?"

I ignored her some more, my temper rising now.

"You have started again! You have started again! Do I have to come home from work every day to come and deal with you? What is the matter with you?"

"You're not the only one who's tired now! I went to school too!"

"Oh, oh, it's me you're talking to like that, *ehn*? Is it me you're talking to like that?"

I could almost see the neighbors on either side of our flat shaking their heads bemusedly, preparing for another late-night show.

For some inexplicable reason, I was not in the mood to let her nonsense wash over me like a sitting duck as usual.

"I can talk anyhow I want, please! Free me!" I said sharply.

"*Ehen*, you're now the mother? I'm now the daughter, so why don't you come and beat me up? Is that not so? Come and beat me up now. Foolish girl, you have no respect for me!"

"As far as I've realized, respect is earned before it is given." I knew I was stoking the fire, but I could not help it today. My impossible Accounting homework had me on edge and here she was, going on about the dirty clothes that were hers!

Mumsie clapped her hands emphatically. "*Ehen*! That's as far as you realize? Who is teaching you that one? Who is the person that is teaching you to talk to me like this *ehn*?"

"Not tonight, please. *Abeg*!" I pushed my workbook closer and attempted to concentrate.

"Not tonight? Anyway, I don't blame you! Please just go and wash those clothes right now if you know what is good for you!"

"I should do what?" I asked as laughter threatened to erupt from my throat. There was no way I had heard her correctly.

"You heard me. I said, go and wash those clothes now!"

She had to be joking. At nine o' clock in the night when the power was out? Head to the backyard to begin washing clothes that I would then have to stay up to dry because I could not leave them out overnight for fear of them getting stolen? Yes, she had to be joking.

"It's late and I have to go to school tomorrow."

Her voice took on a taunting pitch. "*Ehen*? It's now you know that one. That one doesn't concern me *o*. Just go and wash those clothes for me, my friend!"

"No, I have—"

"I don't want to hear *pim* from you again! I don't have time for your madness this night! Go and wash those clothes now!"

"Do you think Popsie would let you treat me this way if he was here?"

She laughed in malice. "Don't ask me *o*. If you like, you can carry your legs to *obodo* London, and go and ask him there. Didn't they tell you they don't want you? You don't know you're not good enough for them? Too much story is not good, *biko*! *Abeg*, go and wash those clothes! I'm tired of talking."

She always did that, used Popsie's new family to taunt me, as though it did not hurt her as much as it did me. Her spiteful comment made me lose what little hold I had left on my temper. "How won't you be tired after you've finished sleeping with all those men at work? How won't you be tired now? No wonder Popsie left you and he—"

A sharp, hard slap from the back of Mumsie's hand extinguished my tirade.

I squealed as she shouted in fury, "Are you mad? Wait, have you lost your senses? Is it not me and you in this house again? You must be a mad woman! You must be on drugs to open that filthy mouth of yours and talk such rubbish to me! You're very crazy, yes! These wings that you've grown, you want to take them and fly, *ehn*? It is a lie *oooo*!"

I flinched repeatedly as she held on to me and rained a couple more slaps on every part of my body she could reach.

Next door, Mama Caroline called out, "Take it easy, *nne*! Take it easy!"

Like she cared. This was only going to be gossip fodder for the neighbors for the next day and a half.

"It...is...a... lie!" A blow punctuated each word. "It's a lie *o*! You hear me? I say it is a lie! I did not kill my mother so you will not kill me! Abi *nwam nwanyi*, do you hear what I am saying? I say you will not kill me! I don't blame you! It's your father inside you! It's his evil spirit that is giving you the liver to talk to me like that.

"Let this be the first and the last time you will open your mouth to say such rubbish to me! In your life, don't you ever, ever, ever talk to me like that again in this house! Come on, get out of my sight! You filthy, bloody fool!"

Tears spilled down my stinging cheeks as I packed up my books and made my way to my room.

"You demon, where do you think you are going?" Mumsie yelled again. "Will you get out of here and go and wash those clothes before I use my hands to kill you and cast you out to Lucifer this night, you this Jezebel?!"

Crying hard now, I bundled up the clothes and headed downstairs.

"Sorry *ee*!" Mama Caroline muttered as I passed by their living room door. Her two youngest children were standing by the door, their wide eyes staring at me shamelessly.

More tears blurred my vision as I lathered up to begin the wash. In a short while, I felt, rather than saw, Tracy join me.

Tracy was the daughter of the neighbor who lived opposite our flat. She lived with an evil single mother too. She understood.

Rage and embarrassment threatened to overwhelm me as I splashed the dirty water on the ground and refilled the basin with clean water for rinsing.

Without a word, Tracy began to help me spread the wrung-out clothes on the line to dry. My bitter tears streamed into the basin of rinsing water as she hummed off-key the opening bars of the hymn 'It Is Well'.

CHAPTER SEVEN
Bibs

...THAT WAS A LUSH SHOWER, yum! I do love the feel of water on my skin. Every morning and night, I stretch out my stay in the shower, to Amina's annoyance.

I can't help it. I feel the steaming hot water flow over my skin, and it feels like I'm cleansing not just my body, but the depths of my soul too. I might never be able to wash myself clean enough but never let it be said that I didn't try.

"BIBS!" I HEAR MY HALF-sister, Amina, call. "Aren't you done yet? What are you doing in there?"

"The day isn't running away, relax!" I cry back from inside the bathroom.

"But time is going! You need to hurry up before Alhaji changes his mind! You know how long it took them to beg on our behalf before he agreed to let us go."

I pop my head around the bathroom door. "I'm out of the shower. Are you happy now?"

"Very!" she replies caustically.

"I'll get dressed now and we'll be on our way."

"Bibs, don't take another year getting dressed! There's nobody there for us to impress!"

Ignoring her rhyming protests, I retreat into the bathroom to pull on my clothes.

I take care not to dress up in front of anyone for fear of discovery, you see. I should stop cutting myself but then, what do I do when I need to run away from *myself*?

Shaking off my unexpectedly dismal mood, I weave my hair into a thick braid.

Alhaji, surprise of all surprises, has given Amina and I permission to go check out the new mall, Value District, which opened down the street from Mega Plaza a couple of weeks back.

There has been a moderate buzz created around this mall because it is the first in the country to have a MacDonald's and a New Look clothing store. It is also rumored to have an official Apple store debuting soon, among other new offerings. For my part, I am mostly excited by the description of the bookstore, cited to be the largest in Africa.

It does feel like everyone in the world, but Amina and I, has checked out Value District. Amina had applied pressure on Alhaji through her mother to let us go check it out too. Alhaji had been in a good mood all week, having successfully closed an important business deal. So not only had he agreed, he had even given us extra money to spend, something he rarely did.

I pin up my braid and call out for Amina, who is impatiently waiting downstairs and then, we slip past the ever-watchful eyes of Abu who hates to let me out of his sight. He can cry for a good clip of time if he sees me escape his clutches.

The driver races to the mall in record time. Luckily, it is not of those bad days where we get stuck in the traffic on the Island for over three hours.

"Yes!" Amina shrieks as we hop out of the car. "We made it!"

"The mall was never running away, you know." I tease.

"Do you know how embarrassing it was to have to hear everyone in class go on and on about this place, and me not being able to chime in because I hadn't been yet? There's going to be no more of that now!"

I chuckle to myself. That is the sort of thing Amina cares about. I, on the other hand, couldn't care less. I am primarily interested in the potential treasures I can dig out of the bookstore.

"It's all good. So, what do you want to do first? Check out the bookstore?" I can foretell what her response will be.

"What?! Who comes to a mall and goes to the bookstore? Lebiba, please! Can't you keep your head out of a book for once?"

"Ha! So, what do you want to do?"

"First, we must check out New Look, of course! Then I want to check the jewelry store on the third floor. Did you know Yemi's mom owns it? We need to get food—"

"Food! Amina, we ate before we left the house!"

In the end, we agree to go our separate ways and meet up in the next hour and a half to decide our next course of action.

I spend my hour and a half exploring every nook and cranny of the bookstore where I snap up a couple of books for myself and Lara who, like me, is an insatiable reader. I also check out her mother's newest interior design collection which is being exhibited in one of the furniture stores on the second floor.

Her mother has an incredible eye for detail and color which I envy. I love design and I am rather handy with a needle. I doubt Alhaji would ever let me go to a design school though. I would not even dream of asking, you see.

As I walk out of the store, I feel someone pull me to a grinding halt. I spin around in surprise and to my consternation, find myself facing Femi.

Femi is a nuisance from school who insists on making my life miserable every chance he gets. He acts like he never left kindergarten. If he is not pulling on my braid like a nursery schoolboy one day, then he is telling me the day after that I made a special feature in his dream. Stupid, pervy stuff like that and it gets on my last nerve.

I am generally solicitous of other people, you see. Fola calls me the resident Mother Theresa. I can't make out half the time if she is being facetious or not. Femi is the one person I cannot be bothered to extend the courtesy of respect to. I cannot stand him and surprisingly for me, I have no problem showing it, although as mildly as I can.

He grabs my hand now and is refusing to let go. "Wow, Lebiba! What's going on? I wasn't expecting to run into you here. How far?"

"Can you let go of my hand, please?" I attempt to pull my hand out of his. People touching me without my permission agitate me.

He tightens his grip and laughs. "Ah-ah, how far? You don't want to say hello?"

"Femi, please let me go. What's your problem?" I bite out icily. It is bad enough putting up with his nonsense at school but not outside it too?!

"You're my problem." He tugs at my hand.

"I'm not playing around, Femi! Please let go and leave me alone!"

"Come and have a drink with me now."

"No! Femi, leave me alone!" I wrench my hand from his and make to push past him, only for the idiot to push me back rather forcefully.

That makes me panic, and the fact that it does makes me furious, angrier than I have been in a long time. My hands are trembling. I hate confrontation, you see, but Femi has crossed the line.

"Don't touch me again!" My voice is trembling too. "Is this a joke to you? Get out of my way!"

"Ah-ah, chill out! Why are you going bananas?"

"Can you get out of my way, please? I don't have time for this."

"I don't have time for this!" He repeats mockingly, planting himself in front of me and crossing his arms across his chest obnoxiously with a provoking leer on his face.

I inhale sharply, never wanting so badly before to hit someone and extra hard at that. I will never know if I would have screwed up the courage to do so because Dimeji intervened at that exact moment.

I close my eyes in mortification when I hear the latter's voice say amusedly, "Simply because there is a seeming disregard for the laws against sexual harassment in our beloved country does not mean you can get away with it, Femi...what's your last name again?"

Oladimeji Young. My ex-boyfriend. Yes, ex-boyfriend. Little old me had had the nerve to date a guy for all of two months in our first year of A-Levels. I had developed a raging crush on him from the word go...crush at first sight. Turned out he had had a super raging crush too; one he had no trouble making known. Long story short, I had given in to pressure from the girls and agreed to date him. Big mistake.

The first time he had tried to kiss me, I had gotten cold feet. While I liked him a lot, I just...had not been able to, you see. The thought of being physically intimate with anybody, never mind that it was only kissing, had made me feel sick.

The second time he tried had been just as bad. No sooner had he drawn me closer and kissed me than I panicked. I ended up pushing him away violently.

Things had become undeniably awkward between us after that, even more so with my clamming up despite his insistent attempts to find out what exactly he had done wrong. We had broken up after that with extraordinarily little to say to each other since.

And now here he is, clearly as droll as he has always been.

Femi scowls at him. "What's your business here, Captain Save-A-Ho?"

"Say one more word and you'll be singing another tune in school on Monday. Now, leave her alone and get lost."

Femi, glowering furiously but too cowardly to take Dimeji on, turns on his heels and leaves. I let out the breath I did not know I was holding. I could not have handled another scene.

"You sure know how to pick them." Dimeji comes closer to me, sounding too amused at my expense.

"What do you mean?" I eye him, disgruntled. "I didn't ask for him to get on my case."

"Do you ever?"

"What?"

"Never mind. You're the last person I expected to see here." He falls into step beside me as I make my way to the escalator to find Amina.

"Why is that?"

"From what I remember, your dad never lets you go anywhere."

"Great, a new expert on my father reporting for duty!"

"Wow, a whole new attitude, huh? What did you do – sink the old one and borrow Lara's?" He laughs.

So not funny. And I tell him so.

"I'm sorry. Let's kiss and make up! No, wait, I forgot. You don't do that either!"

He did not just go there!

"You're coming through with the jokes, aren't you?" I say peevishly.

"Don't mind me, I'm fooling around with you. We both know I wasn't good enough for you."

I sigh inaudibly. What does he know? What does anyone know, for that matter?

I flinch mentally as he pulls on my arm now. "Still waters run deep but you've always been too deep for your own good. Are you still drowning alone?"

I study him in surprise.

How intuitive of him, I think gloomily. If he knew how deep my waters ran, he would not be willing to drown in them with me. Nobody would.

Luckily, Amina comes running up towards us then, so I don't have to think up a befitting response.

"Hey, Dimeji!"

I mentally roll my eyes as she beams at him. With a raging crush on him herself, she had nearly worked herself into an apoplexy when we split. I fobbed her off at the time with the flimsy excuse about not wanting Alhaji to find out.

"Did you get everything you wanted?" I ask her.

"Not everything. We need to grab something to eat. I'm starving!" She whines.

I turn to Dimeji. "We have to go. I'll see you around."

"Sure. The two of you, take care."

"Hmm, did you plan to meet him here?" Amina pounces on me as he strolls off lazily.

"Don't be silly. Of course not!"

"Hmm, are you sure?"

"Shut up. Let's go eat!"

"You still like him, don't lie!"

"We dated ages ago, for crying out loud!"

"So, what? It hasn't been that long, 'Biba! Maybe you'll be less intimidated now."

"You don't know what you're talking about."

She really does not know what she is talking about. I am not ready to get involved again with anyone. I am not about to let anyone in, not now, not ever.

CHAPTER EIGHT
Abi

...FOUND OUT AT EIGHT years old that my parents had had me out of wed-lock before they officially got married.

I'd overheard an argument of theirs—this was before Popsie left, before he had it with her BS. As he stormed out of the house that day, he had yelled that the only reason he had married her was because of me.

Remembering that had always filled me with a warm glow. Well, it had until I told Lara about it. She had laughed and called my perspective stupid.

"What's so stupid about my perspective? He married her because of me, not be-cause of her!"

She had given me a weird look as she answered, "Try the perspective of the woman who married him because of him and not you."

I WHEEZED LOUDLY AS I collapsed on my bed. Not only did I have a rather hectic day at school today, but I also had to stick around after school hours for remedial lessons in Mathematics. I was only now getting home at six.

All I wanted was a shower, a snack, and a long nap, all before Mumsie re-turned from work. Maybe I could even complete some homework. I decided post-haste that I was too tired to shower so I slipped out of my uniform instead and made my way to the kitchen to find something to eat.

The contents in the fridge looked wretched—moldy bread, an almost emp-ty bottle of Coke, and a pack of dried raisins that Mumsie used to bake when she had the time. I glanced up at the plastic jar on top of the fridge. Once brim-ming full of *chin-chin*, my favorite baked pastry to snack on, the jar stood emp-ty and forlorn now.

My options were to starve or stroll over to the nearest Tantalizers outlet three streets away. I was craving their coconut rice and charcolit chicken and figured I could use the opportunity to get the groceries Mumsie had been on my case to pick up from the supermarket in the same area.

I opted for the second option—stuffing myself at Tantalizers—after which I headed to the supermarket, spotting Felicia at the counter as I arrived.

Felicia was the cheery store attendant who had had to drop out of primary school to babysit her sister's children. During the day, she was the housemaid-cum-nanny and in the evenings, she worked at the counter here. She was only fifteen. Feeling sorry for her, I made it a point to pass on my old books and clothing to her, all of which she received with glee.

She smiled now and clapped her hands enthusiastically. "Ah, Aunty Abi! Good evening *o*! Long time!"

"How now? How's Victor?"

She giggled shyly at the mention of her boyfriend. "He dey o! He dey read for exams so he no dey too come around."

"How about your sister and her children?"

"Dem dey! My sister suppose done reach here *sef*. I fit help you find *wetin* you want?"

"No, don't worry," I told her. "If I need anything, I'll call you."

"Ah, I dey here for front *sha*."

I picked up a shopping basket and made my way around the small floor plan, hunting for the things on Mumsie's list. I was so engrossed in deciding what brand of custard to buy that I jumped out of my skin when I heard my name.

It was Saint, an older cousin of a friend in my neighborhood, who came around to visit occasionally. He had been trying since forever to get me to go on a date with him, but I had never taken him up on it. Nice guy, big dreams but too rough around the edges for me.

"Saint! What's up?" I greeted him with a small smile.

"I dey o! I just see your backside, so I come follow you, say make I hail."

God, it was one thing for Felicia to talk like that but a potential boyfriend? Err, no thanks!

"It's been a while since we've seen you around. Where have you been? Did you leave for university yet?" I asked.

"Men, my sister, *e* no easy. Up until now, I dey wait my JAMB results, imagine!"

"Wow, that's crazy. Didn't you take JAMB last year?"

He grunted. "My dear, na last year I take am *o*. I done pursue person on top this matter. Nobody dey wey I never call but no road."

"That's terrible!" I shook my head. "What are you doing in the meantime?"

"I dey train under one of my uncles wey get one fabric factory just so money go flow small for my side."

I shook my head again. Saint was a Physics genius who knew his stuff so seeing him frustrated this way sucked, my lack of feelings for him aside.

To quote one of the many online youth activists, the "bureaucratic and peripatetic educational system in Nigeria" felt like it had been set up for most to fail.

Although I was looking forward to finishing my A-Levels, I was slightly, okay, highly anxious about what would happen next. Mumsie could not afford to send me to university abroad, and I did not particularly want to opt for one of the public universities given the falling standards.

So, my choices were to either end up in one of the private universities here that had ridiculously restrictive rules, or have Popsie maybe step in at last and send for me so I could go to school in London or something. I never stopped praying hard for the latter.

"God is in control," I said to Saint now. "Have you seen Josephine?" Josephine was his cousin and the friend who lived nearby.

"I dey *waka* go that side now. She dey house?"

"I don't know. I haven't seen her this week."

"*Na wa*. But how far that matter I dey yarn you now? I dey wait for you *o*."

It was time for the conversation to end. I managed a fake ha-ha and waved goodbye.

I moved towards the counter where Felicia neatly packed up my groceries. The total came to over three thousand naira.

"Thank you, Felicia." I gave her the little change left to keep for herself.

"Ah, Aunty Abi, thank you *o*! Thank you! Make we dey see your brake lights more *ehn*!" She flashed her white teeth at me.

"No problem. Have you read the books I gave you the last time?"

"Ah, aunty, I dey try *o*. E no easy. You see now, six o'clock in the morning *na* when I dey open shop, so before five, I done wake up. I go now dey shop until maybe around eight for night.

"When I finish, I go come home, come meet the children until my sister done *waka* come, maybe around that nine, ten. Then I go cook and do all these other things and before I say make I try read anything, time done go. E no easy *o*."

Felicia could talk the hind leg off a horse. I gently cut her short. "I understand. Do the best you can and let me know if you need anything."

"No problem, Aunty. Bye, bye!"

I made my way out only to promptly bump into someone who was heading into the store in a blind hurry. The bags in my hands tumbled onto the ground.

"I am so sorry, so sorry." I heard a deep male voice say.

I lifted my head to see a tall, sturdily built man who appeared to be in his early thirties. OMG, he looked so much like R.M.D! Richard Mofe Damijo was one of my favorite Nollywood movie stars, and by popular consensus, one of the most skilled and more importantly, handsome.

This guy right here was good-looking with happy eyes and a brilliant smile. He was laughing softly at himself as he deftly retrieved my runaway groceries.

"Are you alright?" he asked as he stood up with my recovered things in his hand.

"Yes, I am. Thank you for picking up my stuff."

"No, thank you. Not every day I run into a sweet thing like you!"

"I'm not a thing!" I said cheekily.

"Feisty too? I like!"

We both laughed. God, he was so cute. Did R.M.D. have a doppelganger running around?

"I'm Jimi Lawanson."

"I don't remember asking—"

"Touché but now, I'm doing the asking."

"Abi. Abieyuwa Omonitie."

"That's a unique one," he said. "So, Abi, tell me, do you live around here?"

"Yes, some blocks away. I came to get some things for my mom."

"Ah, I see. Your eggs appear to be broken so why don't we head in and um, we'll get you some brand-new ones? It's the least I can do."

Without waiting for me to argue, he took my arm and led me back to fetch the eggs. When he had paid for the eggs and the cigarettes he originally dashed in to get, I thanked him and made to leave only to find he had a grip on my hand.

I looked up at him in surprise and he winked conspiratorially. We headed back outside, my hand in his.

"I need to go now." I said once we were on the street.

"Let me give you a ride." He pointed to a dark-blue Benz.

I kept my surprise in check and smiled nervously. "No, but thanks for the offer."

"Why not? Your mother told you not to talk to strangers?" He teased.

"Yes!"

"You think Mother will protest if I ask for your number too?"

I did not know a lot of smooth guys, but he seemed to fit the bill to a T.

"So, if I give you my number, you'll let me go?" I asked.

"If you promise me you'll see me again."

"See you again? Where?"

"How about you find that out when I call you on the number you're going to give me, or don't you have to be on your way anymore?" He flashed me a wicked grin.

Giggling, I did as he asked.

His face was still lit up by that grin as he put his phone away. "There's a good girl."

"You're funny! Thanks again for the eggs."

"That's no problem at all. I'll see you." With one last wink, he was gunning off in his car.

It was barely a minute after he zoomed off when my cell phone rang loudly.

"It's Jimi. I couldn't hold off." His smooth voice oozed through the receiver when I picked up.

"I can see that," I said, smiling.

"You know, Abi, something tells me we're both going to have a good time getting to know each other and I can't wait," he said.

I was cheesing like a clown. "We'll see."

"I'll make sure of it. I'll call you later?"

"No problem. Take care."

"You too, Abi. You take care too."

CHAPTER NINE
Bibs

...BECOME AN EFFORT TO keep my temper in check of late. I've been rather snappy and irritable, ready to lash out like water heated to its boiling point, like a volcano about to erupt. I exert energy trying to regulate my emotions and I'm running on empty.

"A sinful woman is she who lacks control!" Alhaji berates us girls from time to time. The boys skip that lecture while we live it every day.

Abi says she admires my self-control and would like to be more like me. How do I tell her that I learned the hard way, that I would give anything to learn to act on impulse like her?

I SMILE AS LARA MAKES her way over to join Fola, Abi and I at our usual spot under the gum tree. We are almost halfway through our break period and she is only now joining us.

"Wherever have you been?" Fola exclaims as Lara storms up, looking like a thunderous raincloud.

"Mrs. Akinsefunmi held me back, damn it!" Lara says. Mrs. Akinsefunmi is her Physics teacher.

"Why?" I ask.

"Let's just say I didn't quite grasp yesterday's homework," she says impishly.

"In other words, you got a zero out of twenty points?" I tease.

She laughs. "It sounds pretty bad when you put it like that but yeah, you're close!"

"You Science students, I don't know how you do it!" Abi clucks disapprovingly. She is flipping through the *Cosmopolitan* magazine Fola smuggled into class this morning.

Abi and I are the literature-inclined students, you see. We take what the others regard as the easy way out—subjects like History, Government, and Accounting. Fola and Lara are the science geeks—Chemistry, Physics, the boring stuff.

Fola is the brain-smart one of us all. I consider myself rather smart too unless we factor Mathematics into the equation. Lara can be book-smart when she puts her mind to it and Abi, she will tell you herself, has never particularly been cut out for school. She does as well as she does with our collective help and her remedial classes.

"Physics isn't that bad—" Fola begins.

"Shut up!" Lara interrupts. "It is bad, bad, bad! Are you serious? I swear I spend half of the time trying to work out if Mrs. Akinsefunmi is speaking English or not. It's torture!"

"Manny isn't helping you out anymore?" Abi asks.

"Manny is more of a hindrance than any help most times, you know that. I can hardly get anything done when he's around!"

Manny is Lara's *bad-boy* boyfriend. He is a great guy – attractive with a charismatic personality but he is too much for me. He must have signed a pact when he was born to get into as much trouble as he possibly could at any one given time. It is amazing the number of near scrapes Manny has had.

"Is he leaving in January for sure?" asks Fola.

"Yes," Lara drawls. "He's sent his acceptance. It's about time he got serious about life."

I smile to myself. Beneath her 'don't-care' façade, Lara is dreading Manny's departure as they only have a couple more months together before he leaves.

Fola must be musing along the same veins as I am as she quickly changes the subject. "Guess who I ran into the other day in my estate? Tunji!"

"Tunji? Tunji Adebayo?" Lara asks.

"Yes, him!" Fola trills. "Turns out he moved in over the holidays. He looked so good and I think he was flirting, which was weird."

Lara, Abi and I exchange amused looks. Fola has had the biggest crush on Tunji since we've known her. Whenever we tease her, she insists they are only friends.

"Why do you think—" Lara begins but she is cut short by someone calling out. "Hey guys!"

We all whip our heads around to identify the intruder.

Dimeji.

We gawk at him for a bit before Fola belatedly cries, "Hi, Dimeji!"

"Hey, Fola," he replies, "how are you doing? Would you guys mind if I stole Lebiba for a bit?"

"I'm sure we wouldn't!" Lara sniggers as she turns to give me a searching gaze.

I dodge her look and glance at Dimeji, puzzled. What did he want?

"Um, right now?" I ask dumbly.

"Yeah, I wanted us to catch up before we go back in for classes."

"Is everything alright?" I ask again, stalling for time.

"Yeah, yeah," he replies stoically, his expression giving nothing away.

"I'll join you in a second."

He strolls on ahead as my friends pepper me with questions.

"You dark horse!" Lara exclaims.

"You didn't tell us you started talking to Dimeji again. What's going on?" That's Fola.

"I haven't! I only ran into him this past weekend. I'll talk to you guys later," I tell them, moving to join Dimeji who has sauntered off.

"You will talk to us later!" Lara calls out after me.

I let Dimeji take my hand with little resistance as he leads me to the back of the hall, a secluded area restricted to seniors. The secondary school caste system is alive and well.

He pans the deserted space, clears a bench, motions to me to sit, and flops down beside me as I do so.

"How are you doing?" he asks.

"I'm good..." I answer warily.

"Femi isn't on your case anymore, is he?"

He called me aside to ask about Femi?

"No. Not since that day."

"Right, right," he says gruffly.

"Thank you for getting him to leave me alone."

"You don't have to thank me for that."

"I do. He was getting out of control and I didn't know how to handle it."

"Let's not talk about him right now."

Now he didn't want to talk about Femi?

We do not say anything after that. I shift uneasily as his arm brushes against mine. I am suddenly having trouble inhaling.

Finally, he breaks the silence. "Lebiba, I wanted to talk about...man, let me get to the point. You're not dating anyone, are you?"

I turn to him with furrowed brows. "No one that I'm aware of."

"I'm being serious, Lebiba," he says sharply.

"Why do you care? Wait, are you trying to hit on me or something?" The words slip out of my mouth unbidden. Mortified at my unexpected bout of verbal diarrhea, I clap my hands over my mouth.

He apparently is as surprised as I am because for a good clip of time, he doesn't say anything. Then he bursts out laughing. "Wow, I did not expect that."

"Look, I—"

"And you got fussy when I told you that day that you had a brand-new attitude."

"That's not—"

He cuts me short again. "But you're right, anyway."

"I'm lost. Right about what?"

"You're right about me...trying to hit on you although it doesn't seem like I'm doing a good job."

"You're joking, aren't you?" I ask, nonplussed.

"I'm not, Lebiba. Yes, it's been a while since we dated, if we can call what we did then dating, but I'd like us to give it another go."

I stare at him, astonished.

"I know it's a bit sudden," he continues, "but man, the thing is...I haven't been able to get you out of my mind after we ran into each other over the weekend. I've been beating myself up over how I couldn't make us work."

I blush at his admittedly cheesy admission. He has been on my mind all week too—his voice, his eyes (so penetrating, it feels like he can see everything), the way he stepped up for me at the mall...

"I like you a lot, and I don't think I'd be wrong to say you feel some type of way about me too. We screwed up the communication between us the first time, but I say we give it another try and, you know, work at it this time."

I keep my eyes averted from his, my head spinning from the sheer vulnerability.

"Nothing to say?" He prods.

"What do you want me to say?" I refuse to look at him.

"For starters, you could tell me what you think about what I just told you," he says lightly.

"I-I-I d-don't know. This is all..."

"Out of nowhere?"

"Something like that. Dimeji, we dated for only two months when we did, and we haven't spoken to each other properly since, and here you are now claiming to have these feelings for me and I'm not sure what—"

"I'm not claiming," he says firmly. "I do have feelings for you, and I'm sure a relationship between us now could actually go somewhere, as opposed to our first try."

"But—"

"I want us to try again, Lebiba. Let's take a shot at getting to know each other better than we actually did before."

"I don't think it will...what if it doesn't work?"

He sighs. "Lebiba, what if it does?"

I am still refusing to look at him so I am thrown off-balance when he takes my chin in his hand and gently turns my face towards him so my eyes are boring directly into his. I rush to close them before he sees too much.

"Why won't you look at me?" he asks. "Why are you always hiding?"

Does he genuinely want to know? Does anyone? Can he handle it? Can anyone?

"I like what I see, Lebiba. You know I always have. Stop hiding yourself from me."

I let out the breath I'm holding and whisper, "You might like what you see but I'm not sure you'll feel the same way about what you'll get."

There is another long silence after I say that, so I open my eyes curiously.

"Why don't you let me be the judge of that?" he whispers back.

Is he going to...?

I close my eyes again as I feel his lips brush mine. They do not linger and amazingly, to my disbelief, I feel my resistance melt an inch.

CHAPTER TEN

Lara

...AN ONLY CHILD, THANKS to Mom's fibs about Dad and the guys (I'm not bitter...not I, said the cat). I was very much the tomboy too. Unruly boys made up my rat pack and like Georgie Porgie, we took great pleasure in making girls cry (and not by kissing them either).

To me, girls sucked, end of discussion. They would swap secrets, swear never to tell, and turn around to hurt each other with said secrets.

So, I'd been all shades of wary when Fola first approached me after our first class together on my first day at Gatesbridge. It wasn't until she'd introduced me to Abi, who she'd been friends with since their first year of junior high, and to Bibs, who'd transferred to Gatesbridge the previous term, that I had let down my guard and let them in.

Girls rock and now, I swap my secrets with the gang...well, almost all. Some secrets from the past are better left there. The past is past. The future is now and unlike the past, it is safe.

"THERE YOU ARE!" I CRIED out as Bibs walked into my bedroom after knocking softly.

"Hi there! Tell me you've showered."

"Good timing. I just hopped out the shower," I said wryly. "What's up? Did everything go as planned?"

"Yes!" She replied enthusiastically. "Alhaji is out of town, so I was able to persuade Hajia to let me sleep over. In her mind, we'll be studying for our Biology midterm."

"Good stuff!" I raised my hand for a neat high-five.

What devilry were Bibs and I up to now? Nothing out of the ordinary, just an illicit rendezvous I was helping to facilitate.

Dimeji and Bibs recently got back together, her having given in to his persuasive lines after some initial nerves. Unfortunately, due to her Gestapo of a father, it was getting harder for her to find time to hang out properly with her old-new boyfriend after school hours.

So, I took the initiative to draw up a rather brilliant plan if I did say so myself. Modupe and I were at my dad's this weekend, we only needed some pretext for Dimeji to come over so he and Bibs could spend some quality time together.

My brilliant plan was conniving with Modupe's girlfriend, Nkem, to bully him into having an impromptu pool party at my dad's. What better pretext than a pool party, huh?

Luckily, Modupe hadn't needed much convincing. He invited a bunch of his friends and I rounded up the girls, Dimeji (the reason for the season), Tunji Adebayo (things appeared to be steaming up between him and Fola!) and Manny (no kidding, Sherlock!).

Bibs, of course, had to get to mine under false pretenses, hence her telling her mother that she was sleeping over so we could study. We did have a Biology midterm coming up in the next couple of weeks that we needed to study for. So, we weren't exactly lying.

"Where are the others?" I heard Bibs ask as I rummaged through my closet.

"Abi's mom is apparently being a you-know-what today so she isn't sure yet if she can make it. Fola should be on her way though."

"Is Tunji here?"

"Nope but he's on his way. He was going to pick Fola up, but her mom wouldn't let her hitch a ride with him because he was doing the driving. She sounded pissed when I spoke to her earlier."

"I wonder when he's going to ask her out properly. Do you think he's going to?"

I flopped back on my bed and eyed her mischievously. "Girl, let's leave Fola alone for now. We'll tackle her when she gets here. You tell me how it's going with Dimeji!"

She laughed shyly as she unzipped her travel bag. "It's all good, I think."

"Don't hedge!" I flung one of the many teddy bears that littered my bed at her.

She erupted in laughter and ducked. "I'm not hedging! It's going alright. We're going with the flow because I don't want to rush it."

"Yawn. What base are you guys on? First? Third?"

"Lara!" She laughed again. I cocked my right eyebrow. She was laughing too much and too hard.

I rolled my eyes. "You do not play the shy card with me of all people! Give me the good stuff!"

"We haven't had the chance to do much. We chat regularly and—"

"Boring! Wait, wait, please tell me you at least let him kiss you this time!"

"Shut up!"

"Girl, what are you waiting for?" I squealed. "Do I need to tutor you? I don't know that you'll like my lessons!"

"I *won't* like your lessons!"

"Whatever. What base??"

"Lara!"

"Don't 'Lara' me, Bibs. Tell me!"

She flopped down on the bed beside me. "I'm confused, you see. I'm not sure what I'm doing but I am trying my best to not make our relationship be the disaster it was the last time."

"You could start by kissing him, maybe?"

"He's an awesome kisser, for your information and he is, um, good with his hands!"

"You tease! Tell me more!" I crowed.

She blushed and added, "It's surprising that I'm so comfortable with him this time around. And you know what's even more surprising? I'm also not overly worried about anyone at home finding out. In fact, me knowing they will frown on it is pushing me to take risks with him, you know?"

"Uh huh, that's that whole toddler-playing-with-matches-because-mommy-told-him-not-to syndrome," I quipped sagely.

"You would know about that! It's all good, we'll see how it goes. Thanks for coming up with this pool party idea. You're a genius!"

"Don't I know it! And what are best friends for anyway? I got you!"

She squeezed my hand.

I stood up and stretched lazily. "I'm going to go check on the guys downstairs so hurry and get dressed. I'll be back for you and we can go out together."

"I'll do that now."

I sped downstairs and back outside to the guest chalet where Modupe, Nkem, and a couple of others were already tackling the spicy jollof rice—*jerrof lice* as Mr. Monday, my dad's cook called it in that accent of his—and barbecued chicken specially prepared for us.

After mingling with Dimeji and a couple more folks as they arrived, I headed indoors. My bedroom was empty, but I could hear Bibs getting ready in the bathroom. I pulled on my bikini and shuffled over to the bathroom to fetch the earrings I left by the sink after my shower.

I tapped and opened the bathroom door and then, stopped short in shock. Despite Bibs' loud gasp and her quick but belated attempt to cover herself up with her towel, I easily recognized the long, partly healed red and purple angry looking stripes decorating her upper, inner thighs.

I was never one to beat around the bush and so, I asked bluntly, "Whoa, what the hell have you been doing to yourself, Bibs?"

She turned away, flustered. "It's nothing, Lara. Let it go."

Marching up to her impatiently, I snatched away the towel and let go in renewed shock. The patchwork of wounds was more horrible up-close. I could not imagine the torture she had experienced inflicting those cuts on herself. I wanted to hurl at the thought.

She snatched the towel back from me. Almost too calmly, she said, "Now that you've seen everything there is to see, will you let me get dressed?"

Reeling, I left the bathroom without a word.

I was sitting on the bed pensively when she came out of the bathroom fully dressed.

"You're not ready to go downstairs?" she asked in a somber tone.

"Why, Bibs? Why?"

"Lara, I—"

"I'm not judging you, I promise. Just tell me why."

"Why what?"

"I know what I saw. Don't act like I'm blind and stupid!" I said harshly.

She sat beside me and took my hand in hers. "I don't know why. Can you believe that? I genuinely don't know."

"How long have you been doing this?"

"Too long for me to remember," she replied testily.

"Bibs, I don't understand. What could be tearing you apart so much that you would have to resort to this? Can't you see what you're doing to yourself?"

"It's no worse than the cigarettes I keep warning you off, is it?" She attempted to smile and failed.

I repressed a shudder of dread at the tortured look in her eyes. It did not make sense that I had never seen the demons lurking there before. Was I in tune with the girl sitting next to me? Had I ever been? What could have driven my self-controlled, sangfroid best friend to this...I did not even know what to call it...madness? What else did I not know?

"Bibs, you need to stop—"

"Don't even." Her tone was frigid enough to freeze the room.

What was I expected to do or say now? Our friendship manual did not come with instructions for a whopper like this.

Fighting back threatening tears, I asked, "What else don't I know?"

She smiled cynically. "Anything I haven't told you, you don't need to know."

That hurt. That statement hurt, and I knew she knew that because she quickly followed up with, "I love you, Lara, you know that. You're my best friend. You know everything there is to know about me but—"

"Clearly not everything!" I corrected her.

"The rest is not worth knowing! I promise it's not!" She cried out in despair.

The latent desperation in her voice scared me. "Have you tried talking to anyone about it? A therapist or..."

"Would you like me to walk up to Hajia and tell her, 'Hajia, I can't stop cutting myself, please get me into therapy' or what? In this same Lagos we live in?"

"I get it, but can't you talk to me about this? It's me, Bibs."

"Frankly speaking, I'd like to pretend that this conversation never happened, that you never saw anything, and that everything is fine."

"But it's not."

"Do you think I don't know that?" Her voice was louder now and shaky. "Do you think I don't have to wake up to the proof of that staring me in the face every day?"

"What are you talking about, Bibs? Talk to me!"

"I... can't!" A single tear escaped from her eye. "Leave it alone, Lara. I'm fine with playing this game of pretending and pretending that I am not pretending. This is something I have to deal with on my own."

What the heck was she going through? Why had I never seen this haunted side of her before? Was I so caught up with the superficial that I could not tell when my best friend needed me?

The questions raced through my mind, but I was going to have to leave it. She was getting agitated and with the others downstairs, I did not want to ruin the rest of the day, so I let it go.

I threw my hands around her and squeezed her tight. "It's fine, Bibs. I'm sorry for piling on the pressure. I love you and this hurts to see. I feel helpless and that hurts too. I'm not going to act like I understand what could be driving you this crazy but I'm here. I need you to know that, okay? I'm here."

"I'm sorry, Lara, I'm sorry," she cried, wiping away the errant tears. "I love you too, and I hate that you had to see this, but can we not talk about this again?"

"We won't. Not until you're ready."

She exhaled heavily. "It's all good. Is Dimeji here?"

"Yeah, he is."

"Have I ruined my makeup?" She let out a light, embarrassed laugh.

I tried to laugh too. "No, it's perfect."

"He'll be wondering where we are. We should go down."

"You're right. We should."

She hugged me impulsively, and then she smiled in that way she always did—her sweet, too beautiful smile that never failed to put a smile on everyone else's face, a smile that I had never questioned...until now.

I smiled back but as I followed her downstairs, I could feel a chill drape itself around my shoulders and goose bumps erupt all over my skin. I knew the sensation. It was the sensation you got when something had gone horribly wrong, something you knew would never, ever be right again.

Part II: A-tishoo! A-tishoo!

CHAPTER ELEVEN
Fola

...THAT OUR GIRLS' CLUB is coupled up—-Lara and Manny naturally, Bibs and Dimeji unsurprisingly, Tunji and I hopefully (ha, ha!) and Abi...huh. I have a sneaky suspicion Abi is seeing someone new who, for some unfathomable reason, she's hiding from us.

She gets these calls on her phone and refuses to pick up when she's with us. If she does pick up, she'll get all fluttery and come up with some excuse to move away so we don't hear the conversation. She's been rushing home after school and not hanging out under the gum tree like we usually do.

Lara and Bibs think I'm reading too much into it. I bet she's dating that Saint dude and if so, she's right to keep that under covers because she ought to be embarrassed! I'd be embarrassed for her! I'm not a snob but gee, there are levels. I've got my eyes on her and I'm watching closely.

I LOOKED UP WHEN MY cell phone lit up and a number flashed on the screen. My heart skipped a beat. Tunji.

I picked up with a bashful "Hi!"

"Hey, what's up?"

"Nothing much."

"Where are you?"

"I'm at home," I replied and before he could protest, I added, "and yes, I'm heading out to yours soon."

He said drolly, "I see you're already predicting my words before I say them, huh?"

I giggled.

"Did you make it to church?" he asked.

"Nah, my parents went to Ibadan to see Granny, but they'll be back later tonight."

"Why didn't you go with them?"

"To do what? You know I hate going there. It's so boring!"

I loved my maternal grandmother, but she lived in the rural part of Ibadan that was pure red dust. To make matters worse, she refused to use the heavy-duty generator Daddy got her and so, each visit there was spent in dim light and stale, stifling heat. After a recent series of the most dissatisfying trips, Sayo and I had kicked against going any longer.

"Brat behavior!"

"Whatever!"

"*No wahala.* Let me know when you leave."

"Okay, I'll see you."

I was beaming as I hung up and hurried to get ready.

Within the hour, I was teasing him about his unmade bed while he flipped through channels on the television with the remote control.

Tunji and I had begun hanging out a lot more since his family moved into the neighborhood. We had first fallen into a cute routine of taking walks around the estate almost every day after school, and on weekends where we would catch up on everything going on with the both of us.

Then he had coaxed me into coming over to his place in lieu of the walks on weekends. With his annoying knack of shooting down my arguments, he made me seem like the biggest baby when I initially expressed my hesitation at that new, uncharted territory. Of course, I had to go out of my way to prove him wrong. So, each weekend, I laced up my big-girl boots and went over, just like today.

"No, no, we're not watching football!" I whined when he paused on the Super Sport channel.

"I want to quickly check to see who won the game this morning."

"No!" I smacked his shoulder. "Don't annoy me, Tunji. You know how you get when you've got football on your brain."

"Why don't you suggest something to replace it with then?"

I eyed him suspiciously and reached for the remote.

He solemnly grabbed my hands. "Hey, there's something I've been meaning to ask you."

My heart skipped a beat. "Sure, ask away."

He had a weird expression on his face. "What do you think about us?"

My heart did not only skip a beat this time around. It literally stopped for a full second.

We had not had the 'talk' yet, so I was not entirely sure how to respond. I decided to play it safe. Clearing my throat, I said, "We're good friends. I love hanging out with you and we always have a good time so...yes, homies."

"Mm-hmm, cool story." He grunted when I stopped rambling. "We make good friends?"

"That's my opinion and I'm sticking to it."

"Too bad I don't agree."

I cringed. "What do you mean?"

"I don't see us as friends at all, and definitely not as homies."

That got my back right up. He had the nerve to say that when he was the one calling me all the time and inviting me over?

"Hey, I wanted to put it out there so you wouldn't get it twisted."

"Sure, Tunji, I get it. I'm ready to leave, by the way."

To think I had assumed this thing between us was going beyond the friend zone. I was ready to go home and forget that this stupid excuse of a conversation ever took place.

"Where are you going? You just got here!" He reached for me. "You don't want to find out first why we can't be friends?"

I ignored him and reached for my bag. "You know what? I don't care right now."

"You should though, because this is why." He finally got a hold of my hand, leaned in, and kissed me!

I silently screamed and mentally punched the air as my refugee brain cells limped home from their earlier flight.

When he broke off our kiss so we could come up for air, I had trouble refocusing on his face.

"You don't want to know how long I've been waiting to do that." He confessed.

"No, *you* don't want to know how long I've been waiting for you to do that," I told him as he bent over to kiss me again.

How was that for a reason to be back here every weekend without even being asked? The girls were positively going to lose it when they heard about this!

CHAPTER TWELVE

Abi

...A SECRET BOYFRIEND is hard work. It's even harder having three best friends you typically don't keep any secrets from. Jimi isn't exactly my boyfriend yet, but he is intent on making that happen.

He is attentive, much more attentive than all the guys I have dated put together, and I'm sure that's because he's older and more experienced. I am not at all used to having someone be so attentive where I'm concerned but it's nice, I swear to God.

For now, he's going to remain my little secret. I want to savor the knowledge of having him to myself for a while longer given the novelty of him; the novelty of having, for the first time in my life, someone who cares about me as much as I care about him.

I SIPPED ON THE VODKA and orange juice cocktail Jimi had stirred up for me and slowly ran my hand over the Italian leather couch I was reclining on while I waited for him to emerge from his room.

Jimi's crib screamed money. The décor reflected his expensive but stylish taste. While I did not live in the lap of luxury like my friends did, I knew enough to say that like Lara, I was not a fan of the nouveau-riche style.

"People with new money are so crass," she'd said one time, "with their ridiculously designed houses painted in garish colors, their cliché Coach and old-timey Gucci bags, and their offensively obnoxious cars decked out in equally offensively obnoxious colors. Lord, I can't stand them!" We had had a good laugh at her rant.

Jimi was far from that. He knew the value of his money and he spent it with taste.

Since charmingly wooing my number from me when we met at the super-market, he had put in a lot of work in making me his 'girl-to-be' as he playfully put it. It was flattering though the age difference intimidated me.

Eleven years older, he was a good twenty-nine years to my eighteen years. Practically thirty! To be fair, he was not stuffy, not in the way I pictured in my head an almost thirty-year old guy would be.

I had yet to tell my friends about him partly because of the age difference but more because I knew they would disapprove of him and what they would see as his too polished ways and mannerisms. They would think I was being naïve for encouraging what they would also see as slick lines.

I'd been skeptical about his charm at first, thinking I would do myself no favors getting involved with someone like him, but I could not help being taken in by his persuasive nature. He had an understated yet decisive way of selling his point of view until you came around.

I could not help but trust that he meant everything he said because it showed in his actions. We had just met but already, he would not let a day go by without speaking to me at least once. He insisted on picking me up from school almost every day, never mind that I made him wait meters away from the school gate to avoid an interrogation by my curious friends. He would take me to his place and once, we even hung out with his friends at the boat club he was a member of.

He liked to splurge on me – money and expensive gifts. I refused to accept these because they made me feel weird, like I owed him in turn or something. He would get upset about that, but that was the one thing I stuck to my guns on, like Lara would say. He did not treat me like an unwelcome nuisance. He did not treat me like my mother. He treated me like he wanted me.

And to top it all, he was maddeningly handsome and had the most amazing, outgoing, and mischievous personality, if somewhat flamboyant. He knew how to put a smile on my face when I needed it. Given all of this, how could anyone, least of all, me, help falling for him when he himself had declared that he was head over heels?

I reckoned once the girls got to know him, they would like him as much as I did. That would not be until Jimi and I were official, but I had my fingers crossed for that happening in no time.

I looked up as Jimi came bouncing back into the room.

"Baby!" He crooned.

I sat up, smiling. "What took you so long?"

"Sorry, it was an international call. The shipment I've been expecting is over a week late, so I had to check up on that, you know, do some screaming at the people responsible for the hold-up."

"No problem. Is the shipment on the way now?"

He sat down on the couch beside me, giving me a quick kiss on the cheek. "It should be because I threatened to make some heads roll. How was your day, baby?"

I yawned. "Nothing out of the ordinary."

"How's your mom?"

"Who cares?"

"I take it I'm not going to meet her anytime soon."

"Try never! She'll try to steal you away from me or something!"

He threw his head back in laughter. "Let's thank God I'm not on the market for a cougar, right?"

"That's your problem!"

"So harsh. Why don't you come closer and whisper some sweet-nothings in Igbo to me?"

"How many times do I have to remind you I'm not Igbo? Mumsie is. My father's Edo."

"Okay, in Edo."

I snorted. "How about no?"

"Why are you so wicked? *Oya*, have you done your homework?"

"You're beginning to sound like my Popsie," I said impishly. It irked him anytime I made any reference, no matter how subtle, to the age difference between us.

He rose to the bait as usual.

"What do you mean?" He growled, poking me in the ribs.

I doubled over in laughter—very ticklish—and scooted down the couch. He scooted down after me and grabbed me as I tried to escape. I half-heartedly struggled at first but settled down as he dragged me onto his lap.

"I've missed you," he whispered in my ears.

"You saw me the day before yesterday, Jimi," I whispered back. I didn't know why we were both whispering when it was just us two, but it was cute, and I told him so as I scrambled from his lap to sit beside him.

"So, you haven't missed me, Abi?" He turned to look at me. "Who is the younger guy who has stolen your attention from me?"

"I've missed you too, baby. I was pulling your legs." I tried to placate him by putting my arms around him.

"Liar, liar!"

"No, for real."

He was nuzzling my neck now. I closed my eyes as the hairs on my neck stood up at the touch of his light breath.

"Aren't we watching the movie you wanted to see on Netflix?" I managed to ask.

"What movie?" He purred, his lips against mine. He kissed me before I could say anything else.

The heady haze that clouded my senses drowned out the red flags popping up loudly in my head. It wasn't the first time he'd kissed me—-we'd been dating over two weeks—but somehow, this kiss seemed different from the other kisses we had shared, more intense for lack of a better word.

I reluctantly parted my lips as his tongue pressed against them insistently and I gasped for breath when he surged in at my slight surrender. I realized to my surprise that I was enjoying it a little too much.

It's just a kiss. The thought had barely crossed my mind when I felt his hands creep up slowly my chest, beneath my shirt.

"Jimi?" I said his name on a hesitant breath.

His response was to close one hand over my breast. I squealed in surprise and tried to move, only to squeal even louder when he tweaked the tip.

"Jimi?" I called out his name louder this time.

He lifted his head, his eyes unfocused and hazy. "Don't you trust me, Abi? We're not going to do anything you don't want to do."

He had deftly unbuttoned my shirt without my knowledge. He must have done that while distracting me with kisses. I stared down, disconcerted, and snapped the flaps of my gaping shirt from him.

"No!" I said.

"No what?" He queried rather harshly.

"I don't...I'm not sure I want to do this," I said, not looking at him, at the anger I knew would be lurking in his eyes.

"Fine!" He snapped. "Have a nice time toying with my emotions, you hear? Move over, let me start the movie."

"Jimi." I reached for him, but he snatched his hand away and got up to find and fiddle with the remote. The plasma TV flickered to life as the movie commenced.

He came back to the couch with an ugly frown on his face and sat down farther from me than he had been seconds before.

Not wanting him angry with me, it took a split second to decide what to do next.

Breathing hard, I took my shirt off and taking a deep and much needed breath for confidence, I clambered back into his lap uncertainly.

For a horrible moment, it appeared he was going to reject my indirect offer because he stared stonily past me, his eyes fixed on the TV screen.

Then he exhaled. "What? What do you want now?"

That was simple. "Anything," I told him meekly, "anything that makes you happy."

"I don't want to make you do anything you're not ready for, Abi."

"I-I-I know."

He went silent, watching me as I sat, shy and uncertain, balanced precariously on his lap. And then, my head fell back in shock and cautious pleasure as he took my right nipple into his mouth and nibbled on it gently.

Grasping instinctively at his head as he nibbled away through the lacy material of my bra, I let the new sensations overwhelm me and just when I was convinced it could not get any better, he switched his attention to the other one.

"Jimi!" I cried out heatedly, grasping his head tighter as he urged my bra up and off.

He slowly lifted me up off him and set me down on the couch. I had barely gotten my breath back when he climbed astride me and kissed me again. Engrossed in the heated exchange, I did not notice his hand slip down and under my school skirt until I felt the dampness and his probing fingers.

I cried out breathlessly, arching upwards. He kissed me harder as he stroked away slowly.

I should get up. I should move away. I should push him off. But I could not find the strength to protest. I did not even want to.

"You like this, don't you?" He blew into my ears, neither slowing nor hastening his pace.

I was too caught up in the new, strange shivers running down my spine to form a coherent reply.

"You want this, don't you?" He blew again, his fingers moving languorously.

"Jimi, please." My voice came out brokenly as I arched upwards again in pursuit of something I could not yet define.

My breath came in hard, frantic gasps as I grasped what it was my body was anxiously reaching out for, as I felt my entire body shudder and relax.

I lay there, my eyes closed, trying to readjust my shaky breathing. I knew that I had opened a door that should have remained firmly shut but, in that moment, I did not care.

I opened my eyes to peek at Jimi who was half-astride me with a smug and self-satisfied smile lighting up his face.

"Are you shy?"

I felt warm blood rush to my cheeks.

"Don't be. That was sexy." He sat up, pulling me up with him. "Did you like it?"

I lowered my eyes shyly. "Y-yes."

"We can do it again, you know, as many times as you want." He grazed my cheek with his lips and drew me in for another kiss.

The movie played on, long forgotten.

CHAPTER THIRTEEN
Bibs

...WRITHE IN MORTIFICATION whenever I recollect Lara's expression at my...you know. We haven't spoken about it since that day of the pool party and I pray she never brings it up because there's no way to explain it away.

I had a vivid nightmare last night. Yes, yes, I have plenty of those, but this was different, this wasn't a blast to the past.

This was me running from a masked man who had eventually caught up with me. I had stood my ground when he did and tried to rip off his mask, but he had wrested me to the ground before I could. Then, blood everywhere and I woke up in a cold sweat.

What a strange, meaningless dream! I wonder what Aunt Salimah, who claims to be able to interpret dreams, would make of it.

I am tempted to share with Dimeji, but he'll start asking uncomfortable questions.

Speaking of Dimeji, I've been boldly lying to Hajia about having remedial Biology classes (Biology does gets a bum rap) so I can spend extra time after school with my boyfriend. My boyfriend. So strange to write that but now, I can't stop smiling.

I SIT CAREFULLY ON the queen bed and watch as my mother, wrapped in a thick green silk caftan and a matching shawl, rounds off her evening prayers.

After dinner earlier this evening, Hajia had whispered in my ears that she had something important to discuss with me in her room. She would not, however, say what it was about.

I cannot fathom what she has to say to me that is so important, and I feel a keen sense of foreboding as I wait for her to finish.

She is taking advantage of Alhaji's absence—he left on a business trip this afternoon—to talk to me about whatever it is that is on her mind. If he were around, she would not have the nerve to pull me aside this way. Alhaji detests what he calls closed-door conversations. He does not want anyone closing ranks, you see.

Does Hajia know I have been lying about remedial classes? Has she somehow found out about Dimeji? Has Amina let something slip even though she does not know much? Has Lara gone behind my back to spill the beans?

I can't infer anything from her disposition, and I squirm in anticipation as I wait for her to get off her prayer mat.

When she eventually does, she glances over to where my siblings, Abu and Halima, are sleeping before settling beside me.

"Lebiba..." she says daintily, adjusting her shawl.

"Hajia," I answer impatiently.

Hajia speaks so slowly, as if she must savor the feel of each word before she utters it. She is so careful of what she says as if trained to expect dire consequences if received badly.

Years of living with Alhaji will do that to you. He has a way of making anyone afraid of saying exactly what is on their mind in the face of his cutting, brutal rebukes.

"I don't want you to repeat anything that I say to you in this room to anyone." She switches to Hausa now. "If Alhaji finds out that I told you what I'm about to tell you now, you and I will be in trouble. But it is a selfish and uncaring mother who foresees her child's future and does not call on her to prepare."

I roll my eyes discreetly. "Hajia, what is it? What happened?"

To my irritation, she turns her face away and closes her eyes apparently in deep thought. As I study the worn and weary lines etched on her face, my sense of foreboding triples.

For the umpteenth time, I wonder what drove a once exuberant and assertive woman like my mother to marry a domineering and single-minded man like Alhaji, a man who has done little else but break her spirit and crush her dreams.

The woman my mother's younger sister describes to us is drastically different from the woman I grew up knowing. The few times I see Aunt 'Mina—those times are far and few in between because one, she lives in Kano and two, Alhaji cannot stand her—she regales Hauwa and I with almost unbelievable tales of my mother's daring exploits.

Hajia back then, she told us, had been care-free to the point of carelessness. She had a firm mind of her own and was almost always in trouble with her parents and tutors for being too disruptive and outspoken. People used to say then that Hajia lived her life like she was a match set on fire and burning up at the speed of sound.

Then she met Alhaji in her early twenties. Aunty 'Mina claimed that my mother's vibrant personality was the strongest quality that attracted my father to her. I find that ironic because he ultimately stripped her of that personality, molding her into someone else.

I do not recognize the woman Aunty 'Mina claimed once existed. The mother I know now is a dedicated recluse. She never goes out, she has almost completely lost contact with her family and friends, she finds it so hard to connect to her own children, and she speaks only when she is spoken to. That fire she was once known for has long since been extinguished. The match has burned out, it seems.

There is not much to change but I will die before I have a marriage that will change me even more like it did my mother.

Without warning, Hajia opens her eyes and says heavily, "He's back."

My eyes linger on her as I wait for her to expatiate. "Who? Who is back? Alhaji?"

The sadness and pity in her eyes arouse my mushrooming fears. I feel a chill as I brace myself for the answer that I am not too sure I want to hear anymore.

"Hajia, who is back?" My voice is harsher and louder.

"Alhaji Bamaiyi," my mother replies in a flat voice.

I stare at her blankly as a sudden onslaught of horror and nausea wash over me. It is not possible. No, it is not possible. My hands shaking and my eyes blinking furiously, I drag in several deep breaths to calm myself.

"Back where?" I spit out after regrouping.

Her next words undo me. "He came to visit Alhaji twice this week while you were at school. He was here the day before yesterday. He came again this morning before Alhaji left for London."

"What did he come here for?"

"I don't know. Alhaji received him in the study both times and warned that they were not to be disturbed."

I am almost hysterical at this point. "Why would Alhaji receive him now, Hajia? Why would he do that? Why? After everything?"

"Alhaji wants the best for all of us, Lebiba. He is the head of the house and I'm sure he knows what he's doing."

Does she buy that arrant nonsense? Sometimes, I fear she does.

I get up from the bed angrily and move away from her. "It's a lie, Hajia! Even you don't believe that! That's why we're having this conversation in the first place! All Alhaji wants is what is best for him and him alone!"

"Lebiba!" Hajia gasps at my outburst.

I am not surprised at her shock. She has never seen me lose my temper so visibly, if at all. No-one has. Everyone has me marked as the restrained and composed Lebiba. My restraint and aplomb have always been taken for granted. Lately, however, Saint Lebiba has been unraveling and with reason too.

How could this man show his face in my father's house? And how could my father, despite everything, have the stomach to receive him?

"You know it's true!" I rant as I pace around the room. "What does Alhaji Bamaiyi want now? How does he have the nerve to show up around here again after all this time? Has he no shame?"

"Lower your voice, Lebiba! You'll wake Abubakar and Halima up! I told you we can't let anyone hear what we are talking about. This has to remain between us, please!"

I stop pacing furiously around the room, trying to leash my temper. A sickening thought occurs to me as I glance at my sleeping siblings and it sends me flying back to Hajia's side on the bed.

"Hajia! Hajia, he's not here for...for..." Words fail me in my panic.

"I don't know, Lebiba." My mother sounds scared herself. "Let's not jump to any conclusions."

"Hajia, what if...what if that is what he's here for?"

"Lebiba, we're not going to jump to any conclusions. I'm sure Alhaji knows what he is doing, and he will do what is right for all of us."

"No, Hajia! What if he is here for that?" I insist on an answer.

"Then Allah's will be done, my daughter," Hajia says faintly, her eyes trained on the floor.

"No! No!" I revert to English in my anger.

"Lebiba!" Hajia cries out in alarm. "Calm down!"

I lose what is left of my poise then.

"No, Hajia! No! I won't calm down!" I scream at her. "After everything they've done, I won't accept this! It was because Alhaji claimed to be doing the best for me that we are here in the first place.

"He and that bastard have done their worst! What else do they want? They have taken enough already. What more is there to take? Tell me! He wants to come back and take...*la samah Allah*, Hajia! Somebody will have to die first!"

And with that, I storm out of Hajia's room, refusing to heed her call for me to come back and calm down. I slam and lock my bedroom door and do the same with the bathroom door. I collapse on the floor, trembling violently, my breathing laced with anger and something more potent—naked fear.

Why? Why now? What is he doing back here? What can he possibly want? What do they all want? I have not buried the demons yet and here they are, digging them all up again.

I try to pray but am unable to focus so I lift my skirt instead and trace the contours of my self-inflicted wounds, taking perverse pleasure in the sight and feel of the red, faintly etched lines on my inner thighs.

I chuckle mirthlessly, remembering Lara's horrified expression the other day at her house. I am not worried about her telling. I am confident that secret is safe with her.

I won't unravel now. I won't. I won't. I won't. The words echo through my head like a deadly mantra as I prime the blade and strike at myself, blindly, wildly. It seems today it hurts a lot more than usual.

CHAPTER FOURTEEN

Lara

...HUNG OUT AT FOLA'S yesterday and got to arguing about that famous three-letter word—sex. To be more specific, we were arguing about whether or not boys respect girls less once they've gotten in their pants.

Fola and Bibs, in relatively fresh relationships, got deep into the convo. Abi didn't say much. In fact, she seemed strangely awkward, uncomfortable even.

Yelling over each other, we veered from that topic to arguing about whether or not sex was tied to a girl's 'market value' (me: no, Bibs and Fola: yes, Abi: undecided) and then, to talking about sex itself.

I'm still the only one who has had some sexual experience whatsoever, so I got to pontificate as usual to my friends as the credible fount of knowledge that I am. What were their alternatives—saucy Harlequin novels? Our parents? Ms. Edem, our guidance counselor? Ha.

I had indulged in sex (and a catalogue of other habits) early on, wholly up to no good in my adolescent years, I tell you. Poor Mom.

But yep, indulged but never quite enjoyed it, not until Manny. With others, I gave because they asked, end of. Duty called, obligation answered, that sort of thing.

It wasn't until I rewired my mindset that I set the standards higher. With Manny, I give myself because I want to, not just because he wants me to.

Be careful who you learn from, I tell the girls all the time. Duty calls, choice answers. Don't let them ever teach you different.

I WOKE UP GROGGILY and examined my sweat-soaked sheets in irritation.

The past couple of weeks, I had had intense hot flashes in my sleep, waking up in the mornings to find my sheets and pillowcases drenched in sweat. Yeah, disgusting.

There was also the slight but stubborn migraine that refused to go away and now, I was running a slight fever to boot.

My eyes were bleary with sleep, so I lay back and closed them briefly. I still felt yucky minutes later, so I sluggishly dragged myself out of bed for a cold shower. I was expecting Manny and wanted to be ready for when he arrived.

Modupe was in the main den, watching TV as usual, when I walked in.

"Hey, you." I smiled weakly.

"Yo! Manny's here, waiting for you in the other living room." He glanced up. "Are you okay? You look tired."

"Yeah, I'm running a fever, have a bloody headache, heaven knows what else. Not getting enough sleep or something."

"Have you taken anything?"

"Nope. I'll hunt around for some pills later."

"Hmm," he drawled skeptically. "When last did you have a smoke?"

I had to laugh. "Modupe, you're so silly! I haven't had one in a bit."

He raised an eyebrow in disbelief.

"I promise!" I laughed again. "It's been a week and half since my last one. I haven't felt like one lately. You know, maybe, just maybe, I'm getting over the cancer sticks and if that's true, you should be happy about that!"

"We should have you under the weather more often if that's what will do the trick and cure your need for nicotine once and for all."

I stuck my tongue out at him and hurried to join Manny in the other den. He was lying full prone on the large loveseat, a huge frown on his face.

"Hey, babe." I tried to hug him as I sat beside him.

He scowled. "Took your time."

"Sorry, I'm not feeling too good."

"I'm not, either," he said.

The ugly frown made it clear that today was a bad day for Manny. He was in one of his moods and Manny in one of his moods was not a pleasant Manny, to say the least.

I sighed. "What happened, babe?"

"That bloody tyrant! Always on my bloody case!"

The tyrant was his dad.

"What's his problem this time?" I asked, fondling his ears.

"Check this. He's trying to get me to stay with my aunt when we already agreed I'd stay off-campus. He's getting fresh on me, talking about how he doesn't trust me and how I'm too undisciplined and irresponsible to live on my own. Can you imagine the moron?"

"This is your mom's eldest sister who received your admission letter on your behalf, yea?"

"Yes, who is also in her sixties and lives alone. Why the hell would I want to go live with an old schoolmarm? And who the hell is he to call me undisciplined? Has he checked out the correlation between his sex drive and the number of children he has?"

I stifled my laughter. "No need to worry about it. I'm sure you'll get him to see reason."

"It's so annoying. I'm about to call it a day and not bother going!"

"You won't go to college just to spite him?"

"I'm considering that."

"Don't be silly, Amana," I groaned.

"No, I'm serious! Me and you, let's elope, have babies and call it a day."

"Nice try, but no."

"Check it out, babe, we'll run away to Calabar. I've always wanted to live there."

"And eat *edika-ikong* all day, every day, huh?"

"You know it!"

"Are you really considering not going to Austin anymore, you clown?"

"Yes, I am. I hate that he has stepped in and taken over. I got myself into the fucking school! I didn't tell him when I applied and now, the man's acting like this was his grand idea from the start. Screw that! I've got a good mind not to go anywhere. Let's see how he takes that!"

I loved Manny but Lord, he could test the hell out of me sometimes. He hated to face up to his problems, preferring to run. He would choose instead to act out. It did get tiring.

I used to be that way before Mom and I moved back to Nigeria, but I got tired. I got tired of running but Manny? Left to him, he would run and never stop.

Take this thing with his dad. All he had to do was man up and show his dad that he could be responsible and disciplined. He had gone through the whole application process on his own, like he said. But no, he wanted to sound off about his being victimized as usual.

Fair enough, life had dealt him some rotten cards—his mom dying when he was young being one, and having to deal with a philandering, unconcerned dad being another—but he was inclined to play the perpetual victim and I was not having it today.

I rolled my eyes dramatically. "Isn't it about time you grow up, Manny?"

"Grow up?!" He sputtered.

"You heard me, Amana. Try getting over yourself for once!"

"Are you fucking kidding me?" He sat up abruptly.

"No, I'm not. I'm trying to tell you that contrary to what you think, everyone isn't always out to get you and I hate it when you are in that state of mind. It drives me crazy, Amana. Snap out of it!"

"Will you stop calling me that?"

"It's your name. Learn to love it," I said shortly.

"What the hell is wrong with you?"

"Nothing, Manny! I'm giving you the tough love you need. Besides, I'm so not in the mood for this today."

"Yeah? Some girlfriend you are!"

"Don't start! I'm the one with a whiner for a boyfriend!"

"What the fuck is wrong with you?!"

"Can't you stop swearing all the time?" I said exasperatedly.

"Hell no!" he said, equally exasperated.

"Will you kiss me then?" I was tired of arguing.

He glowered at me. "No! Are you out of your mind? You've pissed me off!"

"You'll get over it, won't you?" I wheezed. My head was aching terribly now.

"No! How are you going to be telling me I need to grow up? Where the hell did that come from?"

"Can we not do this anymore?"

"Hey, you started it! You're my girlfriend, and my girlfriend in my corner is what I need right now."

"Sure, but I'm not going to be your personal sob pillow, Amana!"

"Will you stop fucking calling me that? Only my mom got away with calling me that! What the hell is wrong with you, man?"

"She's dead now, isn't she?"

The look he gave me could have frozen piping hot oil. He glared at me that way for several seconds, snatched up his stuff, and left without another word.

I knew I had gone too far but did not bother calling out after him. My migraine had gotten worse and I did not have the strength to deal with the damage I had wrought.

"Where's Manny?" Modupe asked as I skulked back into the main den.

"Gone off sulking, who knows?" I sank down heavily on the couch.

"You two fought again?" he asked knowingly, his eyes trained on the TV.

"Don't you know it?"

He turned around to look at me and frowned. "Not better?"

"Not quite. I need to sleep it off."

"You should take some medication."

"Eh, I can't be bothered right now."

I stood up from the couch, freshly surprised at how tired I felt. I shook my head to get rid of the sudden vertigo washing over me, and I felt the blood drain from my head as I did so. I tried to take a step or two, but my vision blurred over, and I felt myself stumble over something that was not there.

Dimly, I heard Modupe call my name in alarm. The hell...?

I tried to maintain my grasp on reality and take another confident step forward. Later, I would not remember how I lost the fight and fell to the floor in a dead faint.

CHAPTER FIFTEEN

Abi

...HOW LARA AND FOLA ARE so self-assured. They have no qualms clashing with people with a different view or opinion from them.

Like Bibs, I don't like confrontation of any kind, avoidance is more my style.

I wish those two would rub off on me some more. Sometimes, I wish I could just be them.

I STIFFENED AS JIMI dropped down beside me on his bed and attacked my neck with new-found vigor. He had persisted in doing that all afternoon while attempting to teach me to drive his car.

I had protested when he first suggested that I take a turn at driving on our way back from the restaurant where we had had lunch earlier. He knew I would have no way of paying up if I inadvertently crashed the car, never mind that he would have no problem replacing it in a jiffy.

Nonetheless, he had insisted on me driving and had then proceeded to further traumatize me by attempting to kiss me as I tried to keep my nervous hands steady on the wheel and my equally nervous eyes on the road.

Now we were at his place at last in one piece, and he had not let up. He was being unusually clingy today. I did not mind the intimacy since we were unofficially dating but lately, I was feeling the added pressure to go all the way and I did not feel I was ready for that yet.

"Jimi, you need to stop! You've been misbehaving all day!" I grumbled as he blew in my ears, his right hand moving restlessly over my chest.

His left hand joined the other in its rampage. "Like you don't like it!"

"I'm not saying I don't, but can't we do something else for a change?"

"I love doing this!"

"You didn't even ask about Lara!" I attacked him verbally, trying to push his hands off to no avail.

Lara had skipped school the earlier part of the week with no word, leaving the girls and I worried. It turned out she had fainted while at home and had been rushed to the hospital with a slight fever. Diagnosed with malaria (every blasted disease in this country was somehow always traced back to malaria), she had spent a couple of nights in the hospital. She returned to school today, subdued but very much the caustic Lara, to our relief.

"I did, Abi, at lunch. You told me she was recovering and came to school today."

"I told you that? I don't remember...Jimi, stop!"

"What? I'm not doing it right?"

"No, I didn't say that."

"Then relax and let's have a good time." His hand was now moving beneath my skirt.

In no time, Jimi had smoothly deprived me of my shirt and my pink bra. He was now pulling down my skirt which he had already unzipped.

I breathed deeply at my disarray and pushed at him.

"What now?" he slurred, not looking up.

"Let's stop. I'm...tired," I told him, not looking at him.

"You're tired? Are you for real?"

I didn't answer.

"That's not cool, you saying that. Am I doing something wrong? Your younger boys at school do it better?"

"Which younger boys? You know I hate it when you say stuff like that, Jimi! That has nothing to do with anything. I'm tired. We just ate *ah*!"

He jumped up. "Whatever! I guess we won't need these today then."

Reaching into his pocket, he brought out two condoms and tossed them at me. I gawked in disbelief at the condoms, both colorfully wrapped in foil packages and carelessly displayed on the bed where he had tossed them at me.

"Jimi, we won't...ever need those," I told him quietly once I had stolen a few seconds to gather up the nerve.

He flinched like I had slapped him. Recognizing my folly at being alone with an unmarried bachelor in his own space, an unmarried bachelor I was now not sure I knew, I subconsciously poised for flight.

"So, we won't ever need those, right?" he said tightly.

I could sense the curbed aggravation in his voice, and I tried to speak but he stopped me. "You know what, Abi? I don't get you. I don't! I think it's time for you to tell me exactly what it is you want from me because it looks like we're reading from two different scripts.

"I've been over here thinking that you and I were working on a constructive relationship like two grown adults but it's becoming clear that you're a little girl trying to take me for a ride! What's that about?"

"I-I-I..." I tried to say something, but my tongue was glued to the roof of my mouth.

Guilt paralyzed me. Jimi had made no secret of the fact that he liked me and wanted to be with me. He had given me so much in terms of attention and time. Was I maybe being selfish by not reciprocating in kind?

"You need to leave now." He turned to leave the room.

That jolted me to act.

"No, wait!" I cried, jumping off the bed. "Let's talk about this, Jimi."

"What's there to talk about, Abi?" he asked derisively. "I don't have time for this game you're playing with me. I've put myself out there for you. I haven't hidden anything from you, and I've laid myself bare to you. What more do you want? I don't do this with just anyone, Abi, so I don't need you throwing it in my face."

"Jimi..."

"The least you can do to show me that I'm not doing this in vain is to put everything out there for me. This can't be a one-sided relationship, Abi. I care about you, but I have to know that you care about me too!"

"I care for you too, Jimi but I don't know...it's going too fast. I don't know if I'm...if I can. I'm confused."

He sighed. "Look, Abi, if you care about me like you say, it shouldn't be hard for you to give me anything. It shouldn't be confusing."

His eyes pierced mine earnestly as though he was trying to penetrate my soul and I wanted so much to trust him. I had never connected with anyone the way I had with him and I did not want to lose that. I wanted so badly to feel that I mattered to someone, to anyone, but to Jimi in particular.

"I'm scared," I admitted ruefully, looking away.

He clasped my arms gently. "I understand but I'm scared too, Abi. I feel such a great responsibility not to hurt you and you know I would never hurt you on purpose. This might sound like a tired, old line but I truly feel like words aren't enough to express exactly how I feel for you, how I feel about you. That's why I want to show you, but the question is, will you let me?"

I cocked my head and looked into his eyes again. He did not look away and that helped me make up my mind. I nodded slowly.

He moved to swiftly lift me onto the bed. As he took off his clothes and clambered back on the bed, I swallowed my fear and blurted out impulsively, "I love you."

"That's what I'm talking about. Don't be scared." He smiled, brushing my hair away from my forehead.

I held my breath and tried not to panic as he moved up and over me, slowly edging off my skirt and the rest of my underwear until I was naked.

Oh my God. Oh my God. What am I doing? How do I look? Am I really going to do this? Oh my God. Is this really going to happen? I wonder how my boobs look. The ephemeral thoughts flickered through my head as Jimi kissed me fervently—my lips, my ears, my neck, my breasts, my stomach, my thighs, my...everywhere.

Any common sense I had left was washed away as he concentrated his efforts. I tried to modulate my haggard breathing as I felt the looming invasion of never-before explored territory, as Jimi moved in closer, his kisses increasing in fervor.

"Relax!" He grunted as I tensed when he dragged my thighs even farther apart than they already were.

He drove in without warning. The pleasant sensations died an abrupt death and I choked at his brutal entry. I found my voice and cried out as he pushed on further.

He kissed my sweaty eyebrows. "Don't worry. The pain will go away."

He pulled out and then, he drove in again...and again...and again.

It became markedly clear that Jimi was lying to me because the pain did not go away. Instead it got a lot worse. It hurt more and more. I swear to God, it hurt so much.

I was keening in anguish, but he didn't appear to notice. I could do nothing but lie there as he hammered away, oblivious of everything but his pleasure. From his soft, satisfied groans, it was noticeably clear that we were not having the same experience.

The steamy scenes in my favorite romance novels had always described in fanciful detail the endless pleasure the heroine never failed to enjoy after the initial flash of hero-induced pain. Flash of pain?! This pain was never-ending!

I only wanted Jimi to hurry up and get it over with and I exhaled in relief when he let out one last guttural groan and collapsed heavily on top of me.

"Jimi," I whispered. No answer.

I tried again. "Jimi."

Again, no answer. He had fallen asleep.

"I love you," I had told him.

The tears ran down the bridge of my nose and onto the cotton pillow beneath my head as it struck me that he never told me he loved me in return.

All the novel-inspired dreams I had about losing my virginity to someone special, to someone who would make sure he did not hurt me, who would tell me how much he loved me and hold me gently in his arms when it was over, were now just that...dreams.

In less than ten minutes, a part of me I had avidly guarded for years was gone and what was left in its place was aching regret.

The room was strangely silent. All I could hear now was Jimi's light snoring and the sound of my heart splintering into tender little pieces as I stared down unseeing at the two condoms on the floor, both still colorfully wrapped in foil packages and now carelessly scattered on the floor where Jimi had swept them down from the bed in his ardor.

CHAPTER SIXTEEN

Bibs

...AFRAID, ANXIOUS, FURIOUS...tired of being all the above, thanks to the 'good news' as shared by Hajia. No new developments since then but something needs to give, and now.

I HAVE PERSISTED IN telling boldfaced lies to Hajia about having remedial Biology lessons after school to preserve the extra time I spend with Dimeji these days.

The remedial lessons are, of course, me going over to Lara's to meet up with Dimeji and then going off to his place. We remain cautious so I do not run into anyone who could tell on me, but I have begun to throw caution to the wind by letting him take me to the country club or the mall.

Today has been one of those dare-devil days, Dimeji and I having planned a trip to the movies after school. We run slightly late and the opening credits are rolling up on the screen when we walk into the movie hall. We sneak into the back seats, our hands laden with popcorn and soda.

I enjoy the movie considering that there are generous shots of Idris Elba, one of my favorite actors, topless. It makes me more aware of Dimeji sitting beside me who I hope does not notice my halting breath and goose-bumped skin. He is, however, engrossed in checking out the scantily clad beauties onscreen. A little too engrossed for my liking.

After the movie, we stop by at his place where we make out headily before returning to Lara's where one of my father's drivers is waiting for me.

"What did you guys get up to?" Lara asks as Dimeji guns off after saying hello and hugging me goodbye.

I blush. "Not much."

"Lord, Bibs, you're so transparent. Are you going to fill me in, or do I have to threaten you?"

"Hush!" I push her playfully.

She gives me a smug look and I plead with her to let me go. "Let me give you deets later! I need to leave now. It's a quarter to nine. I'll call you when I'm home."

"See time, you done stay for *hia* now. If *oga* dey around, he for vex *o*!" Benson, my father's driver apprehends me about my tardiness as I approach the car.

I cluck my tongue at him. "Hajia is aware that I came here to study so what's your problem? Can we go now, please?"

I jump into the car and settle down to replay Dimeji's kisses on the ride home. He is an awesome kisser and to my bewilderment, I have become comfortable with his touch this time around. It is a new and incredible experience to not have a panic attack when someone touches me intimately.

It is apparent something is up the moment Benson pulls up into our family compound. The security guard and one of the housemaids, who have been chatting by the gate, give me pitying looks as I emerge from the car.

"Lebiba!" The maid calls out. "Where have you been?"

"I was studying," I respond tersely. "Hajia knew where I was. What is the problem?"

"*Na wa* for you *o*. Alhaji is back, and he has been asking for you since. It's like you're in trouble."

"You see am?" Benson feels fit to chip in, to my irritation. "*Na wetin* I tell you?"

I am stunned. Alhaji has been out of town and we were not expecting his return until the end of the week which is why I was unusually daring in going to the movies and taking my time today.

"Didn't anyone tell him where I went?" I ask no one in particular.

The maid boggles her eyes at me as if I have gone cuckoo. "I don't know for you *o*! Go and meet him in the house!"

I roll my eyes and squeeze my palms together for courage, trying to counter the panic spreading through my limbs.

Hajia and Amina are waiting impatiently for me in the family living room when I walk in.

"Lebiba, we've been calling your phone!" Worry is stamped all over Hajia's face.

"I heard Alhaji is back."

"Yes! He finished his meetings earlier than planned today and decided to come straight home," Amina whispers. "He's in his living room and he said you should come to see him once you get back. What took you so long?"

I ignore her and turn to Hajia. "Didn't you tell him that you gave me permission to go for my remedial lessons?"

Amina butts in. "Use your head! She's in enough trouble for letting you go in the first place!"

"I didn't think you would stay out this long," Hajia cries. "Why did you take so long?"

"I told you I would run late, didn't I? We had to study for Economics!"

"Economics? You told me Biology!"

I pause before saying, "yes, yes, I meant Biology."

"Lebiba!"

"Not now, Hajia! Let me see Alhaji first."

I make my way to my father's living room—the grand space no one is permitted to enter unless specially summoned by Alhaji. He has a private living room, a private dining room and a private bedroom, access to which he rotates among the three wives.

I walk in to see him sitting on the expensive three-piece sofa that is the centerpiece of the room. He glances up at me when I greet him and returns to reading the journal in his hands as if I am no more than a fly buzzing impertinently in his ears.

I stand there fidgeting for no less than five minutes, waiting for him to acknowledge me. Anger froths on the inside of me as I clench and unclench my fists repeatedly. The sadistic man is enjoying this.

My skyrocketing fury scares me, you see. I have been one to be on my father's good side, yes, even after...everything. I've always been so calm, so self-possessed, so submissive, so detached.

The insidious change precipitated the day Hajia called me into her room. Now, I am a human volcano in the making, waiting to spurt at the slightest provocation.

My friends have noticed too. I am less willing to put up with nonsense I would have tolerated before, and I am given to losing my temper at the slightest thing. It is exceptionally out of character for me but with the recent emotional upheaval, I have no strength left to be bothered.

I am tired of living up to what people expect of me. I am tired of taking the fall for things that are not my fault. I am tired of living life the way people, Alhaji, order me to. I am tired of having to hide everyone's secrets, including my own, and dealing with the loneliness that comes with the hiding. I am tired and I have had enough.

At last, Alhaji clears his throat.

"Where are you coming from, and at this time of the day?" He is using the quiet, deadly voice that lures people who do not know him well enough into mistaking his calmness for restraint. Under that façade is a skillfully concealed harsh and brutal temper.

I lie without blinking. "I've been at my friend's house. Our teacher asked her to give me remedial lessons in Biology."

"Where are you coming from?" he asks again, standing up slowly.

I watch him in resentment. What more does he want me to say? What does he want to hear? The truth?

"I..."

"Where are you coming from?" he asks yet again, moving closer.

"Biology remedial at my friend's house," I say again.

He smiles and lifts his eyes to the ceiling. "I ask you for the last time, where are you coming from?"

"Sir, I already told you."

In the distance, I hear quick breaths drawn in shock. The household is listening in. That is the norm whenever anyone of us gets into trouble.

I do not see the slap coming. I should have but I did not. I stagger back in distress, my head reeling from the heavy blow.

"You must have lost your senses," Alhaji says coldly. "You challenge me that way when I ask you where you are coming from at this ungodly hour. You whore! You have paid for your wantonness once and yet, you will not learn your lesson?"

My vision doubles and before I can recover, he strikes me again on the other cheek. I bend over, whimpering.

"You have the effrontery to live under my roof and come in at this hour of the night?" He is leisurely massaging his fingers as though it has hurt him a great deal to hit me. "When did I tell you that my house was now a breeding ground for harlots?"

I cower, visibly shaking in fury, my hands on both my red, inflamed cheeks. I am the harlot? I am the whore who has paid for her wantonness?

"Will you never learn your lesson? You have brought shame to this house once before and yet, you will not turn around from your path to Hell! Will you not tell the devil to flee from you? Why do you persist in being his chosen bride? Why do you persist in being his mistress and whore?"

The grandiose hypocrisy of his speech galls me and I see red.

"I... I'm not a whore," I say stiffly, straightening to look up at him defiantly.

His eyes widen in shock. "What? What did you say?"

"I said I am not a whore!" Tears of rage sting my eyes.

"You dare talk back to me?! You dare..."

Before his hand can jerk forward to hit me again, I dart away and snatch up the gold knife lying on the tray of oranges that must have been served to him for dessert.

"Touch me again," I scream at him, "and I will kill you!"

He stops and ogles me, his hand suspended in the air, rigid in disbelief.

The murmurs and sighs of the eavesdroppers on the corridor are much louder. I vaguely hear someone wondering aloud if they should not intercede.

"I will kill you!" I scream at him again.

"Have you lost your senses?" Alhaji chokes out, after gaping like a fish for several seconds. "Have y-you-you gone mad?"

I assuredly have. I do not know how I have summoned the courage to confront Alhaji, with a stray knife no less, but I do know that I have never felt so in control seeing him in a momentary state of powerlessness.

It is a surreal out-of-body experience, like I have stepped outside of myself and am now watching as the stranger that inhabits my body brandishes a makeshift weapon at a father who has never been that.

With venom, I tell him, "Before God and the angels in heaven, if you ever touch me again in this house...if you ever touch me again, I will kill you. I will kill you and dance in your blood, *insha'Allah*!"

I mean every word.

He stands there, helpless to do anything. The expression on his face bear out the fact that he is having trouble believing what is playing out right under his nose.

His eyes darts to the knife and momentarily defeated, he orders coolly, "Get out of my sight. You're possessed. You have gone mad."

"Mad? Look at you, you have not seen madness yet," I tell him in an equally icy tone and with that, I toss the knife on the floor in front of him and hurry out of the room, storming past the audience in the hallway without a word.

My father fails to realize a simple fact—this darkness of mine did not surface today. No, he himself set it in motion. Since he did, it has laid dormant, biding its time and only now manifesting. Even more terrifying, it will not be held back. Not even I can hold the darkness back.

CHAPTER SEVENTEEN

Lara

...RATHER ANNOYING THAT the malaria I just recovered from is trying to sink its claws into me again. What the heck is this feverish feeling?!

I behaved myself and stuck to the regimented cocktail of pills prescribed by the doctor, but the hot flashes and night sweats are back, with a side of nausea. Yet to tell the clan because I categorically refuse to go back to the hospital.

To make matters worse, Manny is not speaking to me still! It's the longest we've gone without talking to each other. This dude hasn't left for college yet and we're already falling apart.

I gave him his space after our stupid argument but after hearing the gist of what I'd said, Modupe had scolded me and asked me to fix things ASAP. What do you know but that I've been trying to call Manny to apologize and the joker won't pick up my calls!!

What the hell does he want me to do? Crawl to him and lick his feet? As if!

God, I miss him.

I SET THE CAR ON CRUISE control and watched in surprise as Abi jumped out of the dark-blue Benz that had just pulled up in front of her house. She walked over to the other side of the car and nervously peered around, before leaning in to kiss the man in the driver seat. I damn near passed out in surprise.

I ducked down in my seat when she pulled back so she would not see me. What on earth was Abi up to and who the hell was that? Fola just might have been on to something going on and on about Abi having a secret lover.

How did I come to be spying on Abi? I hadn't meant to per se. It had started out with me playing truant today and taking Modupe's car out for a drive. *Shhh.*

My parents—Mom for the most part—flat out refused to let me drive, citing the many dangers of the Lagos roads including the horrific traffic and the dangerous potholes. So not fair considering that one, I was a great driver and two, Modupe and Mayode (when he was around) both had their own cars!

Modupe did let me drive his car sometimes but only when the parents were not around and even then, he insisted on supervising me. Very annoying.

Today, however, Modupe and Dad had gone off to play golf, and Mom had a client appointment. Manny was not talking to me, and I was incensed at him for not having bothered to check up on me when I was admitted at the hospital with malaria.

Sure, what I had said to him about his mother had been almost unforgivable but him not reaching out, even after Modupe let him know that I was on my deathbed (I said what I said!), was equally as bad, in my opinion. He had still not called despite my having tried to reach out to him multiple times!

Anyway, since no one was around and I had nothing else to do, I rebelliously took Modupe's car out for a minor spin around Ikoyi. I was having so much fun behind the wheel, maneuvering through the winding roads and somehow, I found myself on the bridge leading to the Marina.

So, I thought to surprise Abi who lived with her mom on Lagos Island but lookie here now, who was dishing out the surprise this afternoon?

I watched as the Benz zoomed off and before she could make her way to the gate of her compound, I accelerated and pulled up in front of her.

"Lara!" She shrieked when she saw me. "Oh my God! You scared me! What are you doing here? Isn't this Modupe's car?"

"Come over here!" I beckoned to her.

She looked around nervously again before coming over to slide into the passenger seat.

"What are you doing here, Lara?" Abi asked me again.

"Never mind that! Why don't you tell me who that guy was?"

"What are you...what guy?"

"Girl, please!" I scoffed. "I saw you! 'Fess up, who was that?"

She sighed. "He's a friend, okay?"

"Sure. And we started hiding friends from each other when?"

"What do you mean?" she said in an injured tone.

"You have never mentioned him to us, Abi! You're kissing a friend who's got such a fancy ride? You better start talking because you're not getting out of this car until you tell me who he is!"

"He's just a friend. What are you doing here anyway? Are you spying on me?"

"Shut up! Like that's all I have to do with my time! I just took Modupe's car out for a quick drive."

"A quick drive and you're all the way here? You're not serious! Does Modupe know where you are?"

"Don't change the subject!" I stuck my tongue out at her. "Who is that guy?"

"My friend!"

"Boyfriend?!"

"Yes, um...sort of. Not really. Kind of."

I gazed at her incredulously.

She sighed again like some old woman on her dying bed. "I don't know what we are, Lara."

"Right. What's his name?"

"Jimi."

"And you've been sort-of, kind-of dating him for...?"

"Um, over a month or so?"

"Wow! An entire month! And you didn't think to mention him to any of us all the while?"

"There was nothing to tell."

"Right. Was that his car? Or his dad's or something?"

She shot me a scathing look. "That's his car."

"Whoa, whoa, hold up! How old is this dude again?"

She stared ahead with a mutinous expression on her face.

"Abi?"

She ignored me.

"Abi?"

"Aargh, Lara! He's...twenty-nine!"

"Twenty-nine!" I huffed. "Who is this guy? Where did you meet him? How are you dating a twenty-nine-year-old you've known for a month?"

"We're not officially dating...we're having something but—."

"Having what?" I broke in, thoroughly confused.

"I'm like his girlfriend, alright? Can we drop it now?"

"No way! You two are not official, are you?"

Reluctantly, she shook her head.

I noted her wringing her fingers, nonplussed.

"Huh, it is what it is. Twenty-nine though? Isn't that pervy? You should be careful with these older guys. I find it odd but hey, you're smart, you should have your head screwed on right, and you can make sound judgments here. I don't want to believe you'll let him groom you to do what you don't want to so like Bibs would say, it's all good!" I concluded my soliloquy with a wise smile which faded slowly as tears clouded her eyes.

"Abi, you're sleeping with him, aren't you?" I asked in disbelief.

The tears brimmed over.

"I didn't want to, I swear to God, I didn't want to." She started sobbing. "But he made such a big deal about him putting his feelings out there for me and me not doing the same. Lara, you don't understand, it hurts! It hurts me every single time!"

"He forces you?" I asked angrily. "Abi, that is not acceptable!"

"No!" She shook her head emphatically. "He doesn't. I keep telling him it's fine, but I didn't know it would keep hurting like this every time."

"I'm lost right now. Didn't you just meet this guy? When did sex come into the picture?"

She sniffed. "We've been...you know, doing it almost every time we hang out but God, Lara, it hurts me every single time and I don't know how to tell him!"

She started crying again.

"I have to admit I don't understand. Why can't you tell him that? You know what? Let's back up. You said you two weren't officially dating so I don't know...why are you even sleeping with him?"

"He was going to break up with me if I didn't! He said he was tired of me stringing him along!"

I choked on air in surprise. I knew Abi to be the naïve type but good grief, not this naïve!

"Abi, that is ridiculous! How was he going to break up with you if you two weren't officially together in the first place? This dude is a predatory asshole!"

"No, he's not!" She wiped at her tears furiously. "He can be intense but he's a good guy."

"Intense is code for 'asshole'! Come on, Abi! What is an older guy like him doing running after a teenager? Is he dysfunctional? If he were a decent guy of any sort, he would not be sniffing around you in the first place, and he sure as hell would not be hurting you physically, emotionally, whatever! You know better, Abi. How the hell did you get yourself into this?!"

"You don't understand!" She cried, her voice rising. "I knew you wouldn't! This is why I didn't tell you guys! Look, this is between me and him. We have an understanding and we will work it out. I—"

The girl was deluded. I had to set her straight. "Work what out? You two aren't in a relationship. What's there to work out?"

"Look, he loves me and—"

"Abi, what is wrong with you? Any fool can tell you he loves you! How hard is that? You should know better than to fall for that! You've known this guy only a flipping month! What, he throws you a token 'I love you' and like a dog without a bone, you jump at that and give it up to him without blinking? How could you let this guy be your first?"

"Lara, I know what I am doing! Jimi is for real. The way you're reacting is why I didn't tell you guys about him! I knew you'd be unreasonable. You don't have to understand but I'm sure we'll work it out. He loves me and that's enough for me, and if it's going to hurt every time we do it, then that's fine because I love him too!"

It was official. Abi was certifiably nuts.

I hissed in growing annoyance and disgust. "You didn't tell us about him because you know this relationship or whatever is BS! Either you're the most stupid person I've ever met, or you truly believe this garbage you're saying."

"Lara—"

"No, Abi, do you! Do what you want. Just for the love of God, please use a flipping condom while you're at it! Because God knows the diseases that..."

Abi exploded at me before I could complete my sentence. "Hey, hey, hey! Do me a favor, Lara, and go to hell! I don't need this crap from you of all people! As in, who are you to judge anyway?

"You're the one who was slutting it up with every Tom, Dick and Harry before your mother dragged you back here like a wild animal! So, don't talk to me as if I'm a fool, do you hear me? Stay out of my business, mind yours, and get off your high horse! Thank you!"

And with that, she stormed out of the car, slamming the door hard.

Whoa! Just...whoa! That was what I got for trying to talk sense into a friend? She had the nerve to drag me when I was looking out for her?

Bristling with barely bridled anger, I clenched the steering wheel as I watched Abi storm towards her gate. The idiot! The stupid, clueless broad! She was as good as dead to me.

I stamped on the accelerator and headed in the direction that would get me out of there fastest.

CHAPTER EIGHTEEN
Fola

...SURVIVED OUR FIRST argument. He was updating me about his aunt. She had recently filed for a divorce from her husband, the ultimate chronic cheater, and he and his family were pleased that she had decided to stop using her children as a crutch for her failed marriage.

I expressed my regret that his aunt had wasted her life with an inexorable man, and then I added that Mommy would never tolerate such rubbish. Daddy would never even try it.

Next thing, Tunji got cross, calling me out for speaking like a child who needed to grow up and be less self-righteous.

As you can imagine, that upset me! I hate that people call me spoilt or insinuate that I'm narrow-minded because I'm lucky enough to have parents who are committed to each other and their children. Am I expected to apologize for that?!

He apologized in the end. He had to if he still wanted a girlfriend!

MY EYES RAKED UNSEEINGLY over my English notes as my attention wandered. We were having a study period in class and Mrs. Ero was supervising so there was zero chance of having any side conversations under her sharp eagle eyes. I chanced a glance at Lara opposite me and another at Abi sitting ahead. Bibs was somewhere at the back of the classroom.

I sighed and wondered yet again what could possibly have led to the dust-up between Lara and Abi. Like, they were not talking to each other at all! Abi was being surprisingly tight-lipped for once and even Bibs, much closer to Lara than I liked to admit, had been unable to get anything out of Lara either. Bottom line, we had never seen Lara so furious and Abi so miserable.

The worst of it was that the tension between the two had spread to us four. Lara refused to hang out with us if Abi was in the mix, choosing instead to kick it with other classmates or hang back in the library. She was apparently not on speaking terms with Manny either and had refused to tell me or anyone else anything about that either.

Bibs was acting weird too. She had a harried, absent look on her face all the time, and she stuck to Dimeji like glue, almost like she was paranoid about him disappearing any second. The few times I tried to tolerate Abi on her own were more than I could handle because she insisted on being a wet blanket. All my efforts to cheer her up were shrugged off so I gave up.

Our poor, old gum tree had been abandoned for most of the week while I'd been left with no choice but to stay stuck like glue to my own boyfriend's side, given that my friends had collectively lost their minds.

I chanced another glance at Lara's unyielding profile and considered daring Mrs. Ero's eyes and passing a note across to her when Ms. Odulami, our class teacher, dashed in.

I started in surprise as she called out my name.

"Yes, ma!" I stood up quickly.

"You are wanted in the principal's office immediately."

Surprised, I made my way out of the class, not heeding the confused looks I knew the girls and the rest of my classmates were shooting at me. I was more surprised to see my younger brother, Sayo, already waiting in Mr. Sasegbon's office when I got there.

My first thought was he must have gotten into some trouble as usual but Mr. Sasegbon proved me wrong by solemnly informing me that Sayo and I were urgently needed at home and that a driver had been sent to take us ASAP. He wouldn't let us return to pick up our things, assuring us that they would be taken care of.

The drive home was a terse and silent one. Sayo, for once, was abnormally quiet with no wisecracks at the ready and I could not stop worrying about what could possibly have gone so wrong at home. My apprehension multiplied when we arrived to see no one around but Mommy's older sister, Aunty Folake, looking unsettled.

"Aunty Folake! What's going on?" I cried as I stumbled out of the car, followed by Sayo. "Where's Mommy?"

"There's no time to explain!" Aunty Folake said brusquely. "We need to go and meet your parents where they are. *Oya*, get back into the car, both of you, let's go!"

"What do you mean? Where are they?" Sayo spoke up.

"*Mo ni ke w'onu moto, eyin mejeji, ma yo mi lenu!*" she said again in Yoruba this time, jumping into the front seat herself.

We did as she commanded and joined her in the car.

"Is something wrong?" I asked as the car started off again.

"*Ko si nnkan, l'agbara Jesu!*" My aunt replied cryptically.

I stopped breathing as the car pulled up in front of our family hospital. Silently, Sayo and I followed Aunty Folake in where we spotted Mommy in the private waiting room.

"Mommy!" I ran to her in relief. I stopped short when I saw the state she was in. Mommy made it a point to look elegant and put-together, especially because her appearance was a huge factor in her job.

That was not the case today. Never had I seen her look so discomposed and haggard. Her hair was in disarray, her eyes bloodshot and teary, and it was painfully obvious that she had hastily thrown on the mismatched *iro* and *buba* that she was wearing now.

At the sight of us, she began to cry big, heart-wrenching sobs that sounded like they were being yanked out of her forcefully.

Frightened, I put my arms around her. "Mommy, please, what's going on? What is it? Why are you crying?"

She kept at it and wouldn't stop so Sayo and I looked to Aunty Folake for an explanation.

"It's your father." Aunty Folake stepped in once it was clear that Mommy was unable to speak.

"What happened?" I asked, dreading her answer.

"He was involved in a car accident this morning on his way to a business meeting."

My hands flew to my mouth as Sayo gasped.

"Is he...? He's not...dead, is he?" I managed to ask in a muted whisper despite the loud, almost deafening ringing in my ears.

"No!" Aunty Folake quickly assured us. "But he's in an extremely critical condition. The doctors are operating on him as we speak. They say he is lucky to have survived the trip to the hospital."

"W-who was driving?"

"Michael, your father's driver. A fuel tanker slammed into the car on Carter Bridge. Michael died on the spot, but your father was evacuated immediately."

"But how did they know which hospital to bring him to?" I asked again.

"God is a miracle worker *o*! Will you believe your father's colleague happened to be in one of the cars held up in the traffic the accident caused? He had gotten out of his car to check the accident scene and recognized your father. He was the one who arranged for him to be brought here and he called your mother right away."

"Oh my days!" I cried in delayed shock. "Mommy, what the...!"

Mommy seemed more composed now as she wiped her tears and hugged me.

"He's going to be fine," she said weakly.

I felt my own tears fall. "Have you seen him?"

"I saw him briefly before he was taken in for surgery. They had to rush him in because he needed immediate attention."

"They are not sure," Mommy went on sadly, "if he's ever going to be able to walk again."

"No way, Mommy!" I cried. "Don't say that!"

"Why do they think that?" Sayo spoke up hoarsely.

"His legs were crushed in the wreckage," Mommy said. The words came out in staccato fashion like she had been programmed. "It took them some time to cut away all the metal and the delay made things worse. We'll know more when he comes out of surgery."

"*Ko ma tii tan o*," Aunty Folake said. I noticed Mommy shoot her a warning look.

"What more could there be?" Sayo blurted out my unspoken thoughts. His eyes were red from trying so hard not to cry.

Mommy hesitated. "That's all there is for now. What we need to do is pray that everything goes well in surgery so we—"

"Seriously, Mommy?" I cut short her attempt to demur.

"*Wo*, Feyi, they need to hear it from you before they hear it elsewhere," Aunty Folake said.

Mommy eyed her in reproach. "I didn't want to bring it up yet, Folakemi, and not here for crying out loud."

"Feyikemi, they aren't babies." Aunty Folake took her arm. "It is better they hear it from you. It'll be worse if the doctor and... those people come out and take them by surprise."

At that, Mommy turned to us with pain and sorrow in her eyes. "You need to understand that nothing has been confirmed yet but...there are some people here claiming your father has...another family."

"Another family?" Sayo repeated.

"I don't understand." I shook my head.

"Another Mrs. Adeyemi showed up here at the hospital before I did," Mommy continued, her voice trembling. "She came with two boys and she claims she is your father's first wife. One of the boys looks to be a little older than you, Fola, and the younger one...maybe a year or two younger than Sayo is."

I stared at her, thunderstruck. "I don't believe you! I don't believe *her*!"

"Ah, Fola," Aunty Folake interjected almost gleefully. "You need to see the older boy. *O jo baba e gan-an!*"

Mommy shot her sister another warning look.

"I'm going to wait in the car," Sayo muttered at the revelation that the older kid was apparently Daddy's body double. He stormed out, the door of the waiting room swinging after him.

"Is this a joke or something?" I cried, my voice rising. "Mommy, have you known about her all this while? I mean, what's going on here? Is this a Yoruba movie?"

Mommy said. "I'm as overwhelmed as you are but we can't worry about that right now. Your father's health is our priority. This is not the time or place for anything else."

"But wait, how did she find out about the accident? How did she know which hospital he was taken to?"

"This is their family hospital and so, Dr. Abiodun knows her, which is another shocker. He was the one who called her when your father got here."

"Dr. Abiodun knew about her? Is she here now? Where is she?" I asked angrily as tears threatened again.

Mommy couldn't meet my eyes as Aunty Folake snarled. "She's in the other waiting room with the doctors, waiting to receive your father after the surgery."

"What is she doing there?" I was outraged. "You should be the one waiting to receive him! You're his wife!"

"As far as she's concerned, she's his first wife and she's the one Dr. Abiodun had sign the consent forms for the surgery," my aunt said.

"And you allowed that?"

My mother grimaced. "Fola, I told you this is not the time or place to deal with this. My main concern right now is your father."

"You're letting her take your place? Why would you do that? Are the children going to take our place too?"

"Stop it, Fola! Don't make me more worked up than I already am. Why don't you calm down?"

"Calm down?" I shouted. "Calm down? You're telling me that the man I call my father, the man who calls me his first daughter, his first child, has been lying to me, lying to all of us for eighteen years, and you're asking me to calm down?"

"Fola, this is not—"

"I should calm down? I don't think so!"

"Fola—"

"Wow, I can't...Is this some sort of crazy dream because I'm ready to wake up? And if it's not a dream, can he die already, you know, so I can get out of here?"

"Stop that right now, Fola! Stop it!"

"No, don't tell me to stop! He deserves to die for this! You know he does! How could he? He should die for this and I don't care if he does!"

She slapped me. Right there, Mommy hit me for the first time in my life.

I closed my eyes briefly at the impact, then opened them so she could see the hurt and disbelief in my eyes which were streaming anew with tears.

"Why would you slap me?" I asked her shrilly. "Why? Am I the one who lied to you? Am I the one who hurt you? I'm not the one. Daddy hurt you, not me."

"Fola, I'm—"

"No! Don't tell me you're sorry!" I screamed at her. "I don't want to hear it! I meant what I said about him dying! You think I'm going to claim him as my daddy after this? Screw that, he never acted like one, anyway!"

I did not wait to hear Mommy's agonized cries and my aunt's worried pleas. I flew out of the waiting room to seek refuge with Sayo in the car. For once, it appeared like my brother and I were on the same side of the fence. He held my hand and stared stoically ahead as I cried my eyes out.

CHAPTER NINETEEN
Lara

...IN SHOCK. FOLA'S DAD is in unbelievably bad shape at the hospital and from what we've pieced together, he may never walk again! What the heck?

Fola is understandably in no place to receive calls, so we haven't spoken to her at length. All we can do is wait and pray...

IT WAS A STRUGGLE TO open my eyes, but I succeeded and found myself staring into the worried eyes of my parents. Mom's eyes were bright red from crying and Dad's forehead was creased with multiple frown lines.

I turned my head slowly to my left side to see a doctor squinting at something above my head and looked down to see that I was in a hospital bed and not my bed like I had initially thought. What on earth...?

The first sight of the needle disappearing into my arm triggered me into hastily sitting up and trying to remove it in confusion. Did they not tell anyone around here that I'd rather a bullet than a needle?

A nurse appeared from the background. "Lie down," she said kindly. "It's alright."

"What's going on, Mom? Where am I?" I asked, not liking how weak my voice sounded.

"Lie down, Lara," my dad said in a strained voice. "The doctor is checking up on your vitals."

"What? No!" I cried. "What am I doing here? Get this needle out of my arm!"

"The needle is attached to your IV, Lara." The doctor stepped forward, handing her notes to the nurse who silently faded away. "Now, I want you to calm down and we'll tell you what's going on."

Hesitantly, I lay back and closed my eyes hoping to clear what felt like dusty cobwebs in my brain.

"Lara, I need you to open your eyes for me," I heard the doctor say. She was a middle-aged woman with a soothing voice.

I did as she asked, and she peered into them with her ophthalmoscope.

"Right, we are good to go." She pulled up a seat. "I'm Dr. Iroh by the way, and I'm your doctor this evening. Your mother found you lying unconscious in your room earlier today. Do you happen to remember that?"

I closed my eyes and tried to replay the day, but it was foggy. What I did recall was trying to pull off my uniform, having just returned from school. My hands had felt like lead and I hadn't been able to get them to unfasten the buttons of my shirt. I also remembered feeling a scorching heat and...that was about it.

I let out an aggravated breath and reached to pull at the needle in my arm again.

Dr. Iroh stayed my hand. "Lara, the needle needs to stay in. You are dehydrated, and we need to get all the fluid we can into your body. Do you understand?"

Did I understand? Was I a baby of five?

"Nuh-uh! I want to go home. Please get this needle out!"

"Honey," my mom said softly, "let's listen to the doctor. We can go home after that but answer her questions first, please."

"I don't remember anything!" I told Dr. Iroh curtly. "Can I go now?"

"According to your parents, this is not the first time you have fainted in the past few weeks. Your brother also noted that you have recently been complaining about a persistent headache," Dr. Iroh said.

I snorted. "Modupe needs to quit the Big Brother shtick! Look, I can explain this. I've cut down on my smoking and I'm probably experiencing withdrawal syndrome or whatever it's called. Now I'd like to go home, please."

"I'm afraid it might be more complicated than that. We have the blood work from the lab tests we ran on you the last time you were admitted here. I was telling your parents before you came round that although you were initially diagnosed with malaria, I did have some concerns which is why I sent the results in for further analysis.

"The full labs aren't back yet but I want to talk to you about the concerns we have. Now, tell me, have you ever heard of the hepatitis virus?"

I looked at her blankly. "Excuse me?"

"Have you ever—"

"I heard you. What does that have to do with anything?"

My mom jumped in. "Why can't you answer her questions without being so difficult?"

"Mom, please!" I rolled my eyes.

"You're making this harder than it has to be for all of us!" She cried.

"Dara," My dad called out to my mom.

"No, Julius!" She shrugged off his restraining arm. "She does this all the time!"

"Give me a break!" I cried.

Dr. Iroh cleared her throat. "Could I suggest something here? It might be better if you two waited outside, Mr. Kharan, while Lara and I finish our discussion."

"We'll do that." Dad agreed without delay, leading Mom out.

I ignored Dr. Iroh and glanced irritably at the needle in my arm once more.

I have nursed a profound hatred for needles stemming from the one time I shot myself up with morphine when I was thirteen. Yes, you heard right—when I was thirteen, I stupidly injected myself with morphine. It was a one-time thing, never to be repeated, if that made it sound better.

I had just turned thirteen, boobs had sprouted out of nowhere, and the guys I hung out with had developed a sickening fascination with the other girls in our homeroom. It was about that time, you know, when girls and boys began to appraise each other as passably tolerable entities and not the unbearable, disgusting toe rags they had been before.

My body had matured faster than my mind and so, my peers' change of opinion had not come as easily to me. Besides, I had already had an illicit taste of what the boys and girls wanted to do at the back of school and was not interested in a repeat.

Long story short, I had become a pariah with no friends. The boys were occupied with their newly discovered wet dreams and I had never gotten along with the girls so they had not been inclined, and understandably so, to let me in on their petty cliques now that I was no longer a member of the boys' club. So, I had rolled solo.

Until Bartholomew.

Barty, or Batty as most everybody called him behind his back, was a weird and reclusive ginger-haired kid that everyone, including me, was petrified of. He was an avid weed smoker. Everybody knew Barty had the best weed. Rumor had it that his dad had been in the supply business before he got locked up.

Barty and I had the same class schedules and had become friends of a sort. We would walk home together after school, and during the weekends, we would hang out in the park behind the community center. He would roll up a blunt, have me take a puff or three, then we would lie back and commiserate about how screwed up the world was while he finished it off. He was not much of a talker, but he listened.

My old friends had thought me weird for hanging with him, but I hadn't cared. I liked Barty. With him, I could get out the dark stuff on my mind and not have to worry about him judging me or thinking I was crazy because hey, he was crazier.

He gained my unwavering loyalty when he said to me once that he would kill James for me if I ever needed him to.

One day, I had told him that I had tried to cut myself several times with my pocketknife to see what it felt like. He had jeered at that, saying he could get me something to get away from myself faster than that.

Faster than the weed too? I asked.

Nothing compares. He assured me.

A couple of days later, we veered off our usual path home from school, heading instead to the park where he brought out the syringes and vials of morphine that he had traded his older brother's PlayStation console for.

He showed me how to pick the vein and solicitously helped me position the needle so that it only pinched some. The morphine hit me like a rush, and I lay back staring at the sky, oblivious to everything.

Too bad the empty euphoria had not lasted long. I had thrown up for hours after I got home. It had felt like my insides were trying to force their way out—altogether a draining experience.

Luckily, Mom and James had stayed out late that night and I had escaped the ordeal with nothing more than huge bags under my eyes the day after. I had never viewed needles the same way since.

"So, Lara," Dr. Iroh briskly interrupted my reminiscing. "As I was saying, we are awaiting the full labs and running some follow-up tests. However, we do have reason to suspect that you've contracted an infection of the liver—the hepatitis B virus infection."

"What?" I stared at her, uncomprehending.

"Yes, the infection of the liver is caused by the hepatitis B virus, which is spread by direct contact with the blood or other body fluids of infected people.

"That direct contact can occur in several ways not excluding unprotected sexual intercourse, injecting drugs or getting piercings and tattoos with unsterilized or used needles, and blood transfusions. In some cases, the source of infection is never known."

I listened wordlessly to her practiced speech as she went on to expatiate. Most people did not know that they had hepatitis B because it often did not display any symptoms. However, I was exhibiting the earlier milder symptoms of viral hepatitis—the headaches, fevers, nausea, and the episodes of syncope.

Usually, the infection was not treated unless it was suspected to be chronic. So it was possible, she explained, that I would have to get a liver biopsy to confirm if my infection was chronic in which case, I would have to begin a drug treatment ASAP to stop the virus from ultimately damaging my liver.

"Wow..." was all I could manage when she stopped speaking. It had just struck me that I had never thought to ask Barty where he had gotten the needles from.

"Now, listen to me." Dr. Iroh took my hand. "It's not all bad news. We have yet to confirm if the infection is indeed chronic and I don't want you to worry about it until the rest of our lab tests come back and we can give you a more comprehensive diagnosis, alright?

"We're going to discharge you today, but we will have you come back in when the additional results are ready, and we'll go from there. In the interim, I'm going to make some recommendations for changes in your diet. That should help you deal with some of the symptoms you've been experiencing. How does that sound?"

I only used that needle one time. I only used it that one flipping time.

"Have you told them?" I asked her, my head whirling.

"Your parents? I've shared a similar summary with them, but we'll be speaking at length shortly once you and I are done here."

I groaned inaudibly. Chronic liver infection? Possible liver failure?

Where could you possibly have contracted the virus? That was going to be my parents' burning question for me. Mom was going to kill me right after she strangled the answer out of me.

I had never told anyone before about shooting myself up with morphine. It had been a stupid act of recklessness in a desperate quest for attention, one that had turned out horribly and that I had tried to quickly forget. I had only been trying to run away from what I was too mortified to tell anyone at the time.

I could not believe I had been so stupid back then. How could I not have asked Barty where he had gotten the needles from? How could I have been so dumb? So irresponsible?

"Shoot!" I said in between heaving in weak breaths. "Shoot, shoot, shoot!"

"Now, calm down. Again, I don't want you to worry too much, not until we have more information to act on," Dr. Iroh said. "Let me quickly speak with your parents and then, I'd like all of us to regroup on the interim steps I mentioned, okay?"

"Sure, thank you," I replied her with a calm I was definitely not feeling inside.

Shortly after she left, the door to my hospital room opened slowly and someone peeped in, someone with a very worried expression on his face.

Manny.

At the sight of him, I let go of the sobs I had stoically been holding in since Dr. Iroh uttered the word 'hepatitis'. He rushed to my side in dismay.

"I'm sorry!" He was saying over and over again. "I'm so sorry! I'm the biggest asshole for not calling back. I'm so sorry. I love you, babe, I'm so sorry."

"Amana, I'm crying! I don't cry, like ever, but I'm crying now, Manny! I'm crying!" I sobbed as the news sank in.

He held me silently as I broke down. There was nothing he could have said to set my now upside-down world back on its axis. I cried, and buried somewhere on the inside, some little lost girl was crying too.

CHAPTER TWENTY
Bibs

...YET ANOTHER NIGHTMARE featuring a chase by the masked man.

Scrutinizing myself in the bathroom mirror as I brushed my teeth, I wasn't sure I recognized the strange, new light in my eyes, almost frightening in its manic intensity. Where am I disappearing to, I asked my reflection, and who is this taking my place?

I cut myself tonight with a ferocious recklessness bordering on insanity. I was semi-bluffing when I taunted Alhaji about his not having seen madness yet but now, I am not so sure that's true. I am not so sure anymore.

I SMILE AS DIMEJI WALTZES into the room with freshly micro-waved popcorn and two cans of Coca-Cola. "I can see you've got your own personal cinema going on here. How many girls have had this treat again?"

He laughs as he settles on the bed beside me and leans forward to turn up the volume of the flatscreen TV.

"Is that a trick question?" He replies. "You know any answer I give to that will raise *wahala*!"

I push up on my arms to stuff some warm popcorn in my mouth, cheekily sticking my tongue out at him as I do so.

I lack the words to describe how easily Dimeji has become my second skin. It defies reason, you see. I have found that I become a whole other person when I am with him. I become the bolder alter-ego I did not know I had. He represents a fleeting chance at normalcy for me, one I never thought I would have, and I am damning the odds to grab at that chance because I do not know when I will ever have at it again.

"Whatever!" I say to him. "Don't act like you haven't brought other girls in here."

"I don't bring just any girl in here."

"I suppose I should feel flattered then."

He glowers in feigned annoyance. "You could act like you know how to appreciate a compliment for once."

"Hey, pick one! The old Bibs you dated or the Bibs you are dating now!"

"I'll stick with this one right here. You've become rough around the edges but better that than the old prude!"

"Shut up!" I toss a pillow at him. I lean forward and kiss him bashfully on the cheek, stifling a frustrated sigh when he does not take the hint to kiss me on the lips. Do I have to stick a sign on my forehead screaming for him to kiss me?!

Since we began dating again, Dimeji has remained overtly courteous. He rarely makes the move to touch me until I blatantly show him that I want him to. Not that I blame him, he is being careful not to scare me away considering how skittish I was with him in the past.

His patience is wearing thin on me this evening. A couple of scenes into the movie and he is sitting up on the bed, though I am reclined invitingly.

"So... are you going to sit up throughout the movie?" I ask.

"What? Yeah, I'm good this way," he answers, reaching for the popcorn at the same time I do. I notice he snatches his hand away before it can brush mine and I watch, amused, as he takes a lengthy gulp of his drink.

"Wow, are you that thirsty?" I ask sarcastically.

"Lebiba, do you talk this much when you're watching a movie?" he asks as he shifts away to slouch against the headboard.

If he would take into consideration that I would rather be doing something else other than watching a stupid movie now! I bite back the thought and whisper, "Oops, sorry!"

Three more scenes drag on after which I cannot resist letting out a loud yawn.

He eyes me exasperatedly. "The movie's not that boring, is it?"

"I don't know. I'm not getting into it. Are you?"

"You were the one whining about how you had to see it once it was released on Netflix."

"It's not as interesting as I thought it would be."

"It is. You're not following! Focus!" He glues his eyes back on the TV screen.

"Whatever." I mutter sulkily, rolling my eyes discreetly. Why was he finding so hard to take the hint?!

I glance at the clock. I need to be home by eight and it is already six-thirty. I lied to Hajia again about having a study session after school hours. Lara helped me forge yet another note from our teacher in case Alhaji asked for proof this time.

Not that he had said a single word to me after I brandished a knife at him. He left for Kano the next day, was away for a week and a half, and had proceeded to thoroughly ignore me since he returned.

I am not so stupid as to think that is the end of the matter. If I know my father well, he is devising the cruelest way to deal with me in his own time, one that will take no prisoners. In line with my new Wonder Woman persona, I do not care. Right now, I choose to live in the moment with my boyfriend.

I glance in annoyance at said boyfriend who is taking yet another long gulp of his Coke. His eyes are still fastened on the screen.

"Are we going to get around to making out anytime soon?" The acerbic words slip from my lips before I can squash them.

Dimeji, halfway through yet another gulp, sputters and chokes.

My newly found courage flees, and I blush. "Forget I said that! I was playing around!"

"Yeah right you were!" He cracks up.

"It's not funny!"

He cracks up again. "You are the one claiming to be playing around but yeah, I'd rather be kissing you than watching the movie."

"Why are we watching it then?"

"Lebiba! You asked to see the movie! Am I a mind reader?"

"I don't know...I thought Netflix and chill was still a thing." I blush again.

"Tell you what, why don't you come sit on my lap and we can argue about that when the movie's over?"

I move to sit on his lap but instead of settling down to watch the movie like he expects, I take the bull by the horns and kiss him softly.

The stupid boy takes over the reins eagerly and before long, our soft kisses get more heated and I am breathing out quiet, little whimpers.

"Sorry if I'm being noisy." I moan as he blazes a trail of kisses down my extra-sensitive neck. He snickers, his breath making me hotter than I already am.

He makes short work of my shirt and in a fevered daze, I watch as he traces, caresses and closes his fingertips about my chest. A muted groan escapes me when he applies more pressure. I am past caring about noise now. I can tell he is aroused too. His frame is tense, and his face set in complete concentration.

Splaying my fingers over his chest, I let him nibble my lips, feeling him tense some more as I pant into his mouth. On and on and on the touching and teasing goes. I am so absorbed in him; I don't take in anything else but his lips and his hands until the latter suddenly leave me.

I feel him tug at my skirt as if asking for permission before he goes any further. I push at him to wait, not wanting him to see my scars.

"The lights," I say, not meeting his eyes.

He blinks, trying to focus. "Wha-what?"

"You should turn the lights off and draw the curtains," I remind him. I make him turn out the lights whenever our clothes come off.

"Oh. Oh! I forgot! Let me get that!" He kicks off a flurry of movement.

I have taken off my skirt by the time he returns to the bed, now in my underwear alone. I climb back onto his lap, my eyes slowly adjusting to the darkness. My breath catches instantly as he closes his hands about me again.

After an eternity of kissing and groping, he lifts his head. "Lebiba."

I frown at the disruption of our flow and try to keep kissing him.

"No, Lebiba, listen. If we go on, it'll be harder for me to want to stop."

"Do you understand what I'm saying?" he says again. "I'm losing it...let's quit while we're ahead."

I draw back then. Dimeji and I always get this far and then I make him stop, you see. Today, I am sure I do not want him to stop. Today, I feel ready.

He has been so gentle and patient with me. He puts how I feel first, and it is a novel experience for someone like me trained to put myself last. I am a different person with him, like the old me never existed.

It is a perverse mirror of how I feel when I cut myself—I get to escape the reality of my life and I get to feel good in the moment. I get to imagine that I am in control and I desperately want to hang on to that.

I want Dimeji to carve and leave his handprints on the canvas of my body, replacing all the ugly, old prints that have marked me without permission. Bottom line, I do not want him to stop and I tell him so.

"I don't mind if you can't stop,"

He chuckles and then asks soberly, "Are you sure?"

I slowly nod.

"Lebiba, are you sure about this? You know we don't have to."

"Are you going to keep talking?" A hint of impatience tinges my voice.

He chuckles again, his hands cupping my bottom. He shifts and his arousal jolts underneath me.

"Just...just don't hurt me please," I whisper. A soft whisper. I am not sure he heard me but then, he whispers back, "I promise."

Kissing me again, he reaches down to unfasten his zipper and grab a condom. He then turns slightly so that I am under him. The fact that we are now naked dimly registers in my mind.

I feel him nudging, probing. I lose my breath and stiffen as he firmly but gently moves into me. There is a slight twinge and I stiffen even more. He stops to kiss me and whisper against my lips, "I promised."

At his reassuring words, I slowly unclench my fingers and toes to let the anxiety drain from my body. I take a deep breath as he draws back and carefully slides in again. I dig my fingers into his back as he moves over me, and gasp in pleasure as he repeats the motion.

His gentle sliding escalates to a more forceful thrusting and he bites my ear as my nails dig deeper into his back and our bodies begin to rock in rhythm for several long, blissful minutes.

This is what it must feel like to be born again, I think fleetingly as I exult in the sudden rush of physical emotion. I put my arms around him as he slumps on top of me after taking care to see that he is not squishing me, and as I hold on to him, I do not want to ever let go.

He exhales. "Man, I never thought I'd see this day."

I am so glad that I did. I smile to myself.

"Are you okay?" he asks, his fingers dancing affectionately against my skull.

"Yes, I am. Are you?"

"Are you kidding me?" I feel, rather than see, his wide grin.

I revel in the rush of emotion sparked by his answer.

There is a pleasant silence which he breaks now. "What are you thinking?"
I do not have to think twice before answering.

"I 'heart' you." I smile as my heart fills up with this new, unfamiliar emotion.

He smiles down at me. "Yeah, me too. I love you too."

Part III: We All Fall Down

CHAPTER TWENTY-ONE

Abi

..."CHRISTMAS IS COMING, *the geese are getting fat. Please put a penny in the* *old man's hat." Jimi recited this absurd rhyme the other day to my delight. I last* *heard it in primary school!*

How is it December already? Exams are right around the corner, let the cram- *ming begin!*

I STRETCHED ON MY BED, yawning. It was almost six o'clock and I was unusually exhausted. A call from Mumsie had woken me up from my short nap. She had called to remind me about an errand and to say that she would be home late from work as usual and not to bother waiting up.

Like I would intentionally do so. I kissed my teeth loudly, my thoughts turning to my friends.

Fola had returned to school but her father remained in intensive care. The news of the accident had stunned everyone. Mr. Adeyemi, of all people? He always appeared vibrant and larger than life, like nothing could ever stop him.

Now, he was lying in a hospital bed with the verdict pending on whether he would ever walk again. He had fallen into a coma after his last surgery, but the doctors had said recently that they anticipated a path to a quick recovery in another week or two.

The impact on Fola was drastic. The passive and lethargic girl we saw now was the shell of our bubbly, unmarked friend.

Her supposedly perfect family had fallen apart to everyone's disbelief. She, Sayo, and her mother had yet to get over the additional distress of discovering that Mr. Adeyemi had another wife and other children—as in, a whole other family—that he had kept hidden all this while.

With her father unconscious in a hospital bed, her family had had to reluctantly unravel the layers of lies—starting with the many 'business trips'—that he had told them over time to keep his secret family under wraps.

The tragedy was eating away at Fola. She attempted to play it off like she did not care but we were not her friends for nothing. We saw what lay beneath the front she put up and it was raw pain.

She was conflicted. She was hurt, embarrassed, and disappointed that her father had turned out to be other than a paragon of virtue and yet, she felt ashamed for being angry at a man who was in a coma and likely to lose his legs.

Her mother was dealing with her own grief, Sayo had clammed up like the typical male, and that had left Fola trying to come to terms with her father's unimaginable deception and betrayal on her own. She was not succeeding, from what we could see.

In other news, Lara and I were still not speaking. Granted, I should not have said some of the things I had to her during our spat, but it was not fair that she had the exclusive luxury of saying whatever she wanted, never mind the consequences.

Who was she to judge me about Jimi? I had never judged her for the rumors of her past exploits prior to her being dragged to Nigeria. I had never judged her for dating someone as crazy as Manny. Why did she think she could judge me?

Thankfully, it appeared we had an unspoken agreement to not let the other two in on the gist of our beef, so I hadn't had to fend off questions from Fola or Bibs about Jimi. Not that they had been in any frame of mind to ask such trivial questions with everything else going on.

Given that Lara and I were not speaking, I had only found out through Bibs about the several hospital trips Lara had made in the past weeks. While Bibs had not elaborated, the trips had sounded more than the usual routine checkups.

Speaking of Bibs, I had briefly eavesdropped on her conversation with Lara about the huge quarrel she had had with her father and how he had not said a word to her to date. That had been astonishing to hear, that she had gotten the balls to stand up to him.

She and Dimeji were going strong. The chemistry between them was palpable and I assumed they were even going the whole nine yards, as Lara would put it. Our innocent, quiet Bibs was perhaps no longer that.

In summary, things had been rough for my friends lately with Fola's dad in a coma, Lara treating a mysterious illness, and Bibs and her father at odds. I could only cross my fingers and hope that things would get back to normal before Christmas.

I was not doing badly myself. Mumsie had been too tied up with work (or so she claimed) to ruin my life, and Jimi and I were doing great, never mind Lara. It still hurt somewhat whenever we...*did it* but I was getting used to it.

I sighed now and remembering Mumsie's reminder earlier, I picked up the shopping list she had left for me. *Detergent. Toilet soap. Bleach. Always. Air Freshener. Sponges. Milo. Milk.*

I stopped, a sinking feeling in my chest.

Always. Sanitary pads.

In an abrupt rush of motion, I snapped up the calendar on the dressing table beside my bed and began flipping through frantically with unsteady hands as I tried to remember the timing of my last period.

As I counted mentally, I struggled to remain logical in the face of blind panic. It could not be what I was thinking.

Jimi and I always used a condom. Besides, I had been under a lot of stress lately. Living with my mother, being torn that I did not enjoy having sex with Jimi as much as I thought I should, the troubles my friends were going through...all that added up was stress enough to account for a skipped period!

It was just the one period unaccounted for. I had no tell-tale symptoms.

It's a fluke. I feel fine, hope reasoned.

It might be too early to tell though, logic argued.

A picture of two colorful foil packages, lying carelessly on the floor unwrapped, floated unbidden into my mind. Oh my God, we had not used a condom the first time!

I cast my mind back. I remembered looking at the condoms he had thrown on the bed at me when I had told him we were not going to need them.

They were the same condoms he had swept onto the floor when I had given in, the same condoms that had stayed on the floor while we had sex, and the same condoms that had remained there long after he had slept off on me.

Panic set in as I tried to regulate my wobbly breathing. I needed to get a pregnancy test kit or whatever it was called right away! I could not go to the supermarket near my house. Felicia, the store attendant there, knew my mother and me. Any talk of me buying a pregnancy test kit would certainly spark off unneeded rumors.

I breathed in and out steadily, trying to abate the panic but it did not subside. If anything, it intensified.

Changing my clothes hurriedly, I snatched up my purse and keys and headed outside to find a taxi. I could not thank God enough that Mumsie would not be home until much later. With any luck, I would be back before she was.

As I walked into the unfamiliar pharmacy the taxi dropped me off at, I felt an acute sense of unreality. This could not be me, Abi, attempting to buy a pregnancy test kit for God's sake! How could this be happening to me?

This did not happen to people like *me*. *This* happened to Bomo, the self-professed school bird who was rumored to have slept with almost every male teacher and student in Gatesbridge. *This* happened to the women who strutted and paraded Lagos' red-district zone, Allen Avenue. Those were the kind of people *this* happened to, not me!

I muttered to myself to relax as I forced back tears. I was worked up over nothing and the test would prove that. It was normal to skip a period now and then.

I wandered around searching for the aisle that held sanitary products for women before I realized that I wasn't sure what to search for. I was the idiot who did not know what a pregnancy test kit looked like!

Again, a sense of unreality pervaded me. This could not be happening.

I jumped, frightened out of my wits when I heard someone say, "Can I help you?"

It was a female store attendant peering at me suspiciously. Did she think I was here to steal Panadol? A headache was the least of my worries.

"No *o*! Err, no. Yes!" I stuttered incoherently.

She frowned at me and made to go off before I stopped her. "Wait, please! Can you help me? I wanted...see, my friend needs..."

She waited, the annoyed expression on her face communicating how much of an imbecile she thought I was.

I took a deep breath and started again. "I... we...my friend thinks she's pregnant, but she's not sure, so she sent me to get something but I'm not the one who's pregnant, so I don't know..."

God, I was rambling.

"Your friend?"

"W-w-who? My friend, yes! She wants to be sure—"

"You're looking for a pregnancy test?"

"Not me *o*! It's my friend but..." I blabbered as she walked over, picked up a box, and slapped it into my hands.

Some thirty-odd minutes later, I was staring blankly at my bathroom wall, waiting for a thin strip to determine my fate. This was what it had come down to.

The instructions stated that the results would take exactly five minutes.

Three minutes, twenty-six seconds. Time was not on my side today.

Four minutes.

Four minutes, eight seconds.

Four minutes, forty-five seconds.

Five minutes.

I inched over to peep at the strip, my heart in my mouth. There was a new bright rose-pink band in addition to the first control band, making two bands.

I was dead. I was SO dead.

I burst into hysterical laughter which turned to dry sobs within seconds. I calmed down and went to fetch the second kit the store attendant had advised me to get for 'my friend' so I could be sure 'my friend' did not get a false positive.

Twenty minutes later, I was staring at a blue control band and yet another bright rose-pink band lying alongside it. I kept staring in disbelief and then, I threw up.

CHAPTER TWENTY-TWO
Fola

...REDUCED TO AN INTERNAL tug of war. I love him and I hate him more.
I see him lying motionless on the hospital bed, and I want to hug and squeeze him until he can gather the strength to hug and squeeze me right back. Other times, I want to smother him with the deathly white pillows beneath his head.
Daddy, how could you, of all people, have done this to me, to us?

THE SENSATION YOU HAD when you had a chair yanked away from behind you without you knowing and you were unable to stop yourself in time from landing on the floor with a big bang? That was my default mode these days.

A month had passed since Daddy had his accident and it still felt like I had been sucker punched. That could be because I did get sucker punched.

Daddy was in a coma. Mommy had the vapors. Sayo was sulking. And I...I was...I was a fractured, disjointed mess. Our perfect family was no more. It folded up one day and refused to come back. Like God decided to smite us for being such a happy family.

The doctors did not understand why Daddy had yet to come round. More than half of the time, I found myself wishing he never would. But if he did not, who was going to clean up his freaking mess?

Mommy had made Sayo and I take some time off school after the accident, but it had not helped much. All I had done was lie in bed and rot my brains out with TV until Mommy came in and made me shower. We would go visit Daddy in the evenings and I would sit in a chair in the private hospital ward looking at everything but the disturbing tubes and gadgets sticking out of him.

We went in the evenings to avoid running into *you-know-who*, after the one time we had gone in the morning only to walk into Daddy's room to see the *other* Mrs. Adeyemi standing possessively by his bed. She was the complete antithesis of Mommy—fat, uncouth, unfashionable, ugly even.

The hag had stared at us, affronted, as though she had any right to be there. Seconds later, Dr. Abiodun had ushered me, Mommy and Sayo out, telling us to return in the evening to avoid "undue conflict" as he had put it. The mornings were hers, the hag had insisted, and she would not have us intruding on her private time with him.

Sayo had staunchly refused to go back since. Mommy had wept all the way home, but she had gone back to the hospital that evening and every evening after that. I could not help but despise her for it.

How could she be so weak? I wanted nothing more than a chance to leap at that old, haggard witch and claw her eyes out but Mommy chose instead to bawl continually like she had not been disrespected enough, like she had not been dealt the height of all insults.

I had gone back to the hospital the following evening after she had begged me to, hating him for every second I had to sit in the chair, trying to ignore the tubes and gadgets sticking out of him.

By and by, when I returned to school, my friends and everyone else were concerned. I tried to act like things were normal, but it was so hard.

"Are you doing alright?" Bibs had asked the one time she caught me alone.

"Yes," I replied abruptly.

"Are you sure?"

I had not responded, staring straight ahead.

"I don't think you are, Fola," she said kindly.

"Why bother to ask then? Don't trouble yourself next time," I had told her as I walked off.

"I miss the old Fola," Lara had said to me another time. We were nestled against each other at the back of our classroom, my head on her lap as she ruffled my hair and gripped my hand with her other hand.

"I miss her too," I said.

I soaked in the quiet that followed and then confided in a shaky voice. "It hurts. It hurts so much."

"I know," she said, "I know it does, Fola."

I had buried my face in her lap to hide my tears.

I had to deal with the others I did not know as well—my classmates and teachers—trying to cash in sympathy checks. Like they were not sniggering behind my back because they thought I had been taken down a peg or two at last.

"I heard about your dad, Fola. I'm so sorry. May he get well soon," Mary said to me one day in class.

"Excuse me?"

She ventured on uncertainly. "Your dad..."

"What about him?"

"I heard he was in the hospital and I..."

I threw my Physics textbook at her. "Come, are you mad? Don't you ever say anything about my father to me, you hear me? Who are you? Are we guys like that? Try and talk to me about my father again and I will scratch your eyes out, you idiot!"

She had gaped at me in confusion—the way I would have gaped at myself had there been a mirror anywhere around—as my friends dragged me away and tried to calm me down.

I had transferred my ire from the man I could not direct it at to the man who did not deserve it.

"I've been worried about you," Tunji told me when he got me alone on my first day back at school.

I stared fixedly at his lips the whole time he spoke. I had lost count of the number of times I had kissed them. Who was to say that another girl had not lost count of his kisses the same time I had? Daddy, Tunji, these men were all the same, weren't they?

"I want you to leave me alone."

"Fola?"

"You heard me, Tunji. Whatever there was between you and me is done so you need to leave me alone."

"Fola, what have I...?"

"Are you deaf or something? Leave me alone, Tunji!" I shrieked, pushing at his chest. Everyone stopped on the corridor to stare at the two of us. I left him standing alone on the spot.

That evening, I had texted Tunji a break-up message while in my father's temporary home. I sat, staring at but not seeing the man in the bed, the man who had taught me to trust that his money would solve any problem I had.

How ironic was it that the one problem his money could not solve was the very one he had created? Who would solve this problem now that Daddy and his money were not as invincible as he had made me believe?

The bitterness and hatred had welled up in me then like the contents of a Coca-Cola bottle waiting to gush out.

My first lady! He would tease me when I was younger, when he had had a semblance of time for Mommy and me before Sayo had come along.

Your first lady? How about Mommy? I had tittered the one instance he lovingly called me that.

Don't worry about your mother, jo! Iwo ni number one mi forever! He had assured me I was his top dog before his business phone started ringing maniacally. He had neglected to mention the boy born mere months before I had.

Shrugging off my dreary disposition, I knocked on Sayo's door now, peeping in when there was no reply.

"Hey," I said.

"Hey," he replied.

"We're leaving for the hospital. Will you come with us?" I asked.

He had looked up briefly but on hearing my question, looked away.

"You should see him."

His response was curt. "Please close the door."

Every evening before Mommy and I set out for the hospital, I would try to coax him into coming. His answer remained the same. I did not know why I bothered. I wondered why I went to the hospital myself.

Mommy was waiting for me downstairs with Aunty Folake. "Is he coming?"

"No," I replied her hopeful question tersely before greeting my aunty.

Dr. Abiodun was waiting for us with his usual grim expression when we arrived. I had come to dislike him intensely since we found out that he had been in on Daddy's double life the whole time.

Two-faced monster, I thought sourly. Charming Sayo and I with his witty remarks and smiling in Mommy's face when he had known the tawdry truth all along.

I lingered behind as Mommy and Aunty Folake moved aside to get Dr. Abiodun's daily update on Daddy's prognosis.

It was the same routine every evening. We would check-in at the reception, Mommy would catch up with Dr. Abiodun and then, we would go into Daddy's room and sit with him for an hour or so. I would leave after the hour was up, and Mommy would depart with Aunty Folake much later.

As I waited for the adults to round up their quiet discussion, I reflected on the incongruous fact that I had seen my father more times in the past month than I normally would have in span of a year. To think that I had once been fine with his long absences, it was pure irony.

A sudden, loud exclamation of agony and despair resonating down the hospital lobby harshly punctuated the stillness of the waiting room.

"Yeeeeee! Mo ku, mo ku, mo ku o! Mo daran oooooo!"

I spun around to see Mommy screaming with Aunt Folake and Dr. Abiodun struggling to hold her up.

"What is it?" I shouted as I ran up to join them. "What's wrong with her? What's going on?"

The pity in Dr. Abiodun's eyes felt like a dagger to the heart.

Less than ten minutes. Internal bleeding. Did all they could. His words came across a jumbled mess as I felt the blood rush to my head.

With Mommy's screams echoing in my ears, I pushed past the somber adults and rushed towards Daddy's hospital room. I could see from the entrance that he was lying in the bed and looked the way he did every evening—motionless, unmoving, dead. Only this time, he did not just *look* dead. He was...

He was gone. Gone.

The nurse swiftly blocked off the door, but she need not have bothered because I could not find the strength to take another step. I felt my legs give way as I crumpled to the floor in a heap.

I could see my sardonic eulogy to him writing itself now—Daddy the liar, the cheat, the coward. The man who never put us first. The man who never put me first. It was work, or money, or the hidden wife, or the hidden children, or business or...gee, dear old Daddy even put death before us. Farewell now, Daddy. Rest in pieces.

Mommy was screaming in the distance. Whatever was she screaming for? He was only gone as usual, no big deal.

I fell apart, sprawled on the floor, as hysteria-tinged giggles erupted violently from my throat.

CHAPTER TWENTY-THREE
Abi

...CONSOLE MY BEST FRIEND over an unwanted loss when I have yet to reconcile myself to an unwanted gain? How do I help my best friend make sense of the chaos in her life when I can't make sense of the chaos in mine?

This has got to be the worst timing for things to fall apart. I am neck deep in exams and cannot afford to fail and repeat the year. But how exactly am I to prepare for these stupid exams with the issue at hand? Where is my Waymaker, abeg?

I HAD HIT A NEW RECORD—THROWING up at least once every other day. At least once every other day! Being pregnant was one ugly, relentless dream I could not seem to wake up from, as hard as I tried.

How could I be pregnant? As in, p-r-e-g-n-a-n-t? As in, something, something alive, growing on the inside of me? I did not feel pregnant. I should have known intuitively if I was, right?

I had examined my stomach critically in the shower yesterday. It had felt as flat as ever (okay, as semi-flat as ever) and it crossed my mind that I might have been paranoid all this time. As if to bolster my line of thought, I had not thrown up once the entire day. I had even relaxed somewhat.

Sadly, the madness had begun again this morning. I felt as sick as a dog and could not stop throwing up. Luckily, Mumsie had had to call into work, so she had not been home to watch me suspiciously hurl out my insides.

If she had been, she would have acted the archetypical Nollywood mother, summoning me to examine my eyeballs and the soles of my feet before spitting out an accusation. Out of an abundance of caution, I had replicated that dramatic examination but since I had no idea what to look for, I had found nothing, duh!

As I recovered now from yet another round of puking, I felt a panic attack coming on. I had been having a lot of those lately. Nightmares too.

In my nightmares, my belly would swell to five times its size and then burst open. I would look down to see a monster tearing its way out with blood splattering everywhere. My mother would then come over and rub dried pepper seeds into my open wounds while my friends gathered around laughing in scorn as I screamed in pain. I would wake up then, sweating and needing to pee. I did not need to be Joseph the dreamer to interpret these nightmares.

The other day in the school library, I had thoroughly confused myself with a furtive Google search for pregnancy symptoms.

Morning sickness? Confirmed.

Fatigue? Confirmed. I was sleeping all the time and had been sent out of no less than three different classes this past week alone for falling asleep.

Peeing all the time? Maybe. The baby would apparently only begin to press down on the uterus between the second and third trimester. I was going to the bathroom more often than usual or was that in my mind?

Spotting? Not sure. Some websites said spotting was a confirmed sign you were losing your baby while others swore it was a sign that you were pregnant.

Two days ago, I had made a trip to the bathroom and noticed blood specks on my underwear. My excitement at my period having finally arrived had been tempered by the fact that there were no accompanying cramps and the blood had been an odd, dark color. I had then convinced myself I was losing the baby but as the day went by, my heart had sunk as it became clear that it was neither of the two options.

I was in full-blown panic attack mode now, thinking of the dizzying list of symptoms I was trying to stay on top of. I wanted to claw at my belly or smash myself against the wall repeatedly until the alien in there was dislodged and came gushing out. I wanted to rewind time and never be in this frightening place ever again.

Jimi, Jimi, Jimi. I chanted his name in my head like a mantra and felt the anxiety gradually subside as I did so.

He was picking me up in a short while. He had noticed that I had been withdrawn over the past week and a half and had been pestering me to tell him what was going on. He was going to get an answer today.

He was on time and in his customary jovial mood. After failing to rouse me out of my sullen mood with his jokes, he stopped at a cafe to buy some ice-cream to cheer me up and we headed to his house. We had not reached the front door when he started pawing me.

I felt myself get angry. Wasn't this the "do-first-ask-later" behavior that had landed me, us, in the predicament we were now facing?

"Jimi, stop it!"

He ignored me, reaching over to unfasten the buttons on my shirt.

"Stop it, Jimi!" I pushed against him as he tumbled us onto the couch.

He did not listen, stopping only to yank down his pants and pull on a condom.

You should have remembered to pull one on back then, I thought dryly.

"I've been thinking of you all day, baby." He grunted as he carelessly pushed into me. I lay there, unmoving, as he moved over me.

Who knew, maybe he could drive out the baby this way? I sniggered wearily as I counted the tiles on the ceiling.

After what seemed like an infinity, he put his clothes back on, pulled down my skirt, and tenderly kissed my forehead.

"I have to make a call, baby. Make yourself comfortable, hmm? I'll be right back," he said.

I closed my eyes and ignored him. I did not remember falling asleep until I felt him shrugging me awake.

"Baby! Did I work you out that much?"

I peered at him blearily as if he were the stupidest person I had ever met. I was beginning to think he was.

"Are you angry with me?" he asked again. "Don't be, baby. I had to make that call. It was important. I'm expecting a shipment from Europe and the guys over there are giving me a hard time, so I had to follow up, you know, same old story. Are you hungry?"

"No," I replied quietly.

"You want to watch a movie?"

I summoned my courage and said in one breath, "No, Jimi, I have something to tell you."

He looked at me quizzically. "What is it, baby?"

I was breathing faster now. "I-I-I can't find my period."

"You can't find your what?" he asked, perplexed.

"My period, Jimi."

Time seemed to freeze as he realized what I was trying to tell him. He gingerly pulled away and studied me as if he were seeing me for the first time.

"What are you talking about?"

"I think I've missed my period!" I cried.

Several seconds passed before, to my utmost surprise, he threw his head back and began to laugh. As in, laugh. As in, a belly-deep, rib-cracking laugh.

"Jimi..."

He continued to laugh, paused to catch his breath and then, he chortled in amusement. "Abi! You're so funny."

"I'm sorry?"

He chortled again. "Your period is missing? It's missing? Ah, what are you doing here then? You better get the hell out of here and go find it!"

I repeated dumbly. "I'm sorry?"

"I said, you better get out and go look for it because you won't find it here."

"Jimi, what are you saying?"

He burst out angrily. "What the hell do you take me for, Abi? A fool? Jesus Christ! I thought you were different, but I should have known better. You've been fooling around with one of your small, small boys, eh? And you think you can pin the result of that nonsense on me?"

I stood in outrage. "Are you out of your mind? How can you say that to me? Which small boys? You're the first guy I have ever been with and you know that! We didn't use a condom the first time, don't you remember?"

He chuckled. "Abi, look..."

"Do you think this is a joke or something? Because I'm not finding it funny! Nothing about this is funny, Jimi! Be serious for once!"

"I'm as serious as a heart attack, my darling. Look here, I'm done having this conversation with you. There's no point to it. Get out of my house and go and look for your missing period. I've told you, you won't find it here!"

He made to walk away, and I pulled him back roughly by his sleeve.

"What do you mean, Jimi? What do you want me to do? I'm telling you that I might be pregnant for you and you're talking to me like this? No, this is not you. This is not the Jimi I know."

"Get real, Abi! What makes you think you know me, huh? You're not my wife, you're not my girlfriend! You're some girl I did a favor and picked up from the street to show a good time, but you are clearly trying to take advantage of that. I thought we had an understanding. Why are you trying to change the game?"

I stared at the stranger in front of me, dumbfounded. I could not comprehend how Jimi, of all people, was in fact denying me and discrediting what we had together.

"Look, Abi, I have a soft spot for you. If you need money to sort yourself out, I can give you some, that's not a problem. Go find a good doctor and have this irresponsible boyfriend of yours take you there and you can take care of this...thing. That's the best I can do for you."

As he spoke, he reached in his wallet and shoved a bundle of naira notes at me. I froze in shock.

"Jimi?" I gasped. "What is this? What are you doing?"

"There's no need to get emotional. Take the money and go and handle your business."

"My business?" I cried. "My business, Jimi? This is our business. I didn't make this...this...thing by myself. Jimi, you can't do this. You know I haven't been with anybody else but you!

"You're the first and only guy I've ever been with. You told me how proud you were to be my first. You told me you would always be there for me. Jimi, please, don't do this, please. I don't...what will I tell Mumsie? What will I tell my friends? What will I do?"

"Why are you asking me? Go and ask your little boyfriends!"

"Which boyfriends?"

"You tell me! You tell me, Abi!"

I studied him incredulously. He sounded so indignant and self-righteous when he knew he was a hundred percent responsible for this. How I had never seen this deceptive side of him before, how I had been fooled into believing the picture of the responsible man he painted for me, the responsible and honest man who meant every word he said to me—I did not know. What I did know was that I had proved myself to be a horrible judge of character.

"I have work to do," he said. "Take the money and leave. Go sort yourself out and don't come back here again. We're done, you and me."

He could not mean that. Leave and go where? Sort myself out where?

I grabbed the sleeve of his shirt angrily and held on for dear life.

"What's the meaning of this, Abi? Let me go!" He demanded.

"No, Jimi, I won't. I won't let you go! Until you admit that you're responsible for this pregnancy, I'm not going anywhere!"

"Abi, let go of my shirt right now!"

"No way! It's Abi now, right? No more 'baby'? No more 'honey'? No problem. It's me and you today!"

"Abi, I'm warning you. Let go now!"

"Do your worst, Jimi! Do your worst!"

And so, he did. He struck me heavily across my face so hard, I literally heard my joints give way as my head spun in the opposite direction.

He did not stop there. No, he pummeled me a couple more times as I recoiled and screeched loudly for him to stop. He dragged me towards the door, smacking me all the while, and shoved me out the door hard enough that I went tumbling down on the concrete floor, bruising my shins.

I stayed down on the ground, my eyes glazing over as he threw some money at me, the naira notes he had tried to give me earlier and yelled at his security guard to make sure I left. He then turned around to go back in, slamming the door shut without a second glance.

It took some time before I was able to stand. Aching from head to toe, I dusted myself off and hobbled my way to the gate to let myself out, leaving the money he had thrown at me on the floor.

I was unable to process the absurdity that was my life—the fact that I was pregnant, the fact that the man responsible had just disclaimed me, hit me and tossed me out, the fact that the man who claimed to love me had turned out to be a monster, the fact that I had been misled by a man that I loved and trusted blindly. I was unable to process any of it knowing that if I tried, I would break down and I could not afford to, not yet.

The tears poured down my cheeks as I sat in the backseat of the car that I had successfully booked via the local ride-sharing service after a delay due to my poor connectivity.

"Aunty, you sure say you dey okay?" The driver kept blabbering as his rickety car sped over the potholes, rumbling and rattling like it was sure to fall apart any given second.

I closed my eyes and shut him out.

Feeling lonely was not new to me. I had felt lonely all my life. I had always been the one on the outside looking in. Loathed by my mother. Unwanted by my father.

My friends had family, loved ones, or money at the minimum. I had always been the odd one out with *no one* and *nothing*. Meeting Jimi had changed that. For once in my life, I had *someone*. At least, I thought I had but more fool me for he had made a fool of me. Once again, I had no one and nothing.

Feeling lonely was not new to me. I had felt lonely all my life but today, I had never felt so alone.

CHAPTER TWENTY-FOUR
Bibs

...OVER THE MOON SINCE I went all the way with Dimeji. Yet to tell a soul, not even the girls. It's a heart-warming secret that has me smiling at the most random of times.

Duty calls, choice answers, it is like Lara says. The freedom to choose has never felt so heady.

I CANNOT BE BLAMED for having remained oblivious to the storm that has been brewing at home. After all, I have been busy with end-of-term exams which are, mercifully, almost over. I do not think I have done a shabby job with them so far but nevertheless; I have been eagerly anticipating the three weeks we get off school for the Christmas holidays.

While my family does not celebrate Christmas, we have been making plans to celebrate the Sallah holiday coming up before then. *Eid al-Adha* is an important holiday in our household, and we have tons of relatives come from out of town to spend time with us.

My thoughts have also been occupied with Fola. The news of her father's death had been devastating to hear. We had known he was critically injured but had not thought his injuries close to fatal. Fola and her family are, of course, broken up about it.

Given the circumstances, she will not be returning to school for the rest of the term. Princi has given her special permission to take her exams after school closes for the holidays. It is such a horrible way to end the first term of our last school year.

Then there is Dimeji. I have been overwhelmingly absorbed with our new physical relationship, using up every excuse in the book to 'study after school' so I get all the spare time I can with him.

I am in love with him, you see. He makes me happy—the happiest I have been in too long and Allah knows I deserve some happy. Thinking about him leaves the widest smile on my face and it is all I can do to not rub it in everyone's faces.

So, with all the above preoccupying my mind, I am taken off-guard when the brewing storm breaks, and with such a vengeance.

I should have known that Alhaji would never let my insubordination slide, but he had maintained his peace for so long that I forgot the man was a patient hawk, swooping on his prey when they least expected it.

And so, my heart freezes and sinks like dead weight to the soles of my feet when Hajia tells me this evening that Alhaji wants to see me in his private living room.

"What does he want to talk to me about, Hajia?" I ask my mother as calmly as I can.

"I don't know," she replies. "He didn't tell me."

"He hasn't said anything to you about that day?" I ask again.

She shakes her head nervously.

I make my way to Alhaji's living room, steeling myself for what is to come, my disquiet growing. How bad can it be? Worst-case scenario, he will have me grounded for the holidays and compel me to attend classes at our Islamic community center every day. I will most likely not see Dimeji and the girls for the three-week period, but they will be there when school resumes. I can live with that.

"Come, sit down, my daughter." Alhaji smiles at me as I walk in to see him partly reclined on his daybed.

He puts down the papers he was shuffling through, takes off his reading glasses, and scrutinizes me critically as I quietly take a seat. My heart has unfrozen and is now throbbing painfully.

"My beautiful daughter." He is still smiling. "You are now a beautiful woman. Who is the man that can resist you?"

I shift uncomfortably under his sharp gaze, a sneaking suspicion worming its way into my mind. Does he know about Dimeji? Has he been having me followed? Has he somehow found out about my 'extra-curricular' activities?

I consider each question, trying to make sense of his overt and suspicious friendliness.

"Fruit of my loins," he says again in Hausa.

I remain silent, my head bowed, refusing to look at the sneer plastered across his wrinkled face.

"Why are you afraid to look at your father? I have good news for you."

I chance a glance at him then. He has paused to sip his whisky.

Seconds stretch before he speaks again.

"I'm confident you have not forgotten your husband."

At the ominous words, I hold my breath as tightly as I can, as my world skitters off its axis. If I let go of my breath, I will crumble to dust. Breathe, Lebiba. Breathe.

"Husband?" I murmur tonelessly.

"Surely it hasn't been that long, has it?" he asks.

There is no mistaking his tone now. It is spiked with malice and unadulterated pleasure at my obvious uneasiness.

I watch him without a word, refusing to come undone in his presence.

"Bamaiyi says he is ready. He's ready for his wife and son to come home."

I refuse to take in, to acknowledge, his horrifying words.

My lack of response does not faze him as he simply goes on. "He will be coming for you before the end of this week so be prepared to leave by then."

I continue to stare at him. This is beyond any and every nightmare I could have imagined. I pinch myself hard and screw my eyes shut to reorient my head but when I open them, it is only to see my hateful father sneering at me.

Quaking with fear, I say vehemently. "No! No, no, I can't...I won't go!"

Midway through another sip of his whisky, he stops and barks, "What?"

Slowly, I go on my knees, tears beginning to pool in my eyes. "Please, Alhaji, please don't make me go. I can't go back there. In the name of God, please!"

"What is the meaning of this? Your rightful place is with your husband and he has demanded that you come back. You mean to defy your husband?"

"Alhaji, please, I beg you in the name of God. I don't want to go back there. Please don't make me go back."

"I have no time for this nonsense. You are now your husband's problem. You and Abu need to be ready to leave within the week. Your mother will help you get ready."

I stand on my feet then. "What about school?"

"That is for your husband to decide. I am starting to understand why some wise men have always insisted that too much education rots the brain. Why else would you have been displaying such lunacy in your father's house?"

This coming from a man furnished with a doctoral degree. My eyes rake over him in amazement and disgust.

"So, this is my punishment?" I ask, my voice wrecked with sobs. "You're sending me back to that monster. You're sending me back to that monster who raped me and got me pregnant. You're sending me back to the man who then disclaimed me and my baby. No! No, no, no! I won't do it!"

How can this be happening? How can my own father think to send me back into the lion's den when I barely survived the first encounter with the beast?

Four years ago, I had only just clocked fourteen when Hajia told me that I had been betrothed to Alhaji Bamaiyi at twelve. He had three wives and many daughters, and I was to be the fourth wife to bear him a much-valued son.

The knowledge of my betrothal had not surprised me, being a family tradition. In our circles, close families preferred to inter-marry for multiple reasons, not the least of which was *keeping the money in the family.*

My grandfather and Alhaji Bamaiyi's father had been best of friends. Alhaji Bamaiyi had also worked for my father, his mentor, before setting up his own successful business. It was easy to connect the dots that Bamaiyi would in time marry into our family.

Two of my older half-sisters (both by-blows) had been married off to Alhaji's business associates. Another half-sister had had the good luck of getting married to the son of Alhaji's good friend and not the aged friend himself. In fact, Hajia Halima, my father's third wife, had been an *arrange-e* herself.

So, the arranged marriage business had not been news to me, you see. Besides, being betrothed did not mean that you had to get married right away. Sadiyat had been betrothed to her husband at thirteen but had not moved into his house until she turned twenty. Medinat's husband had even allowed her to complete a second graduate degree before they officially got married.

I had had a horrifically different experience. Shortly after learning about my betrothal, I had been invited to visit Bamaiyi and his wives at the place that was to become my home in the future, a future I hoped would be as far off as possible if I had my way.

Preliminary visits to the home of your future husband were the norm. The older wives had the chance to dissect their future competition and if necessary, let their husband know if they strongly disapproved of his choice.

My first and last visit had been awkward. I had felt like a coarse diamond being inspected for the minutest flaws.

First had been dinner with the wives and the children—a number of the latter had turned out to be older than I was. Subsequently, I had been driven to Alhaji Bamaiyi's secluded villa where he entertained his important guests.

I curse the day I stepped into that place. He had lured me to the master bedroom under the pretext of showing me around the villa but the second we were left alone, he had promptly asked me to take off my clothes.

Bewildered, I had hesitated. He had asked again, and I demurred—no one had mentioned this part of the script to me. He laughed and asked if he did not have the right to examine what he was paying such a high price for to ensure it was in perfect and intact condition. I demanded to be taken home straight away.

I have spent too many nights following that day trying to forget what had followed that childishly haughty demand.

The end of my innocence had begun with a violent slap that had sent me flying halfway across the room and had ended with the most brutal violation. I could not help but cringe whenever I recalled the sound of my thin, reedy voice desperately begging him to stop, desperately begging him to let me go to no avail.

It was over before I knew it and just like that, Bamaiyi had ripped all sense of control from me, a false sense of control, I had later come to realize because in truth, I had never been in control from the day I was born as my father's daughter.

And afterwards...afterwards, he had stood over me with this look of sheer disgust on his face. Even now, I can only picture what I must have looked like lying there on the bed, my hair an unruly mess, my eyes bloodshot, my arms bruised from where he had grabbed and held me down, my legs splayed open, something wet and sticky trickling down my thighs.

It was only after struggling to sit up that I had realized the wet and sticky stuff was blood. Oddly enough, I had not panicked at the sight. In fact, I had felt irrational relief. The blood was proof that this was real, that this had happened.

"Get yourself together and stop lying there like a harlot!" He had snapped harshly as I sat there, staring dumbly at the blood seeping through the sheets. Of course, I was the harlot.

He made me shower, fetched a maid to get me clean clothes, and he had brushed my hair himself, kissing my forehead and telling me what a good girl I was. My response had been a muted shudder.

Nobody had suspected a thing when Alhaji Bamaiyi brought me home. My empty eyes, my slightly disheveled state, my halting pace, and my listless mood should have triggered an alarm, but my family had long since grimly adopted their roles as champions of denial.

I had locked Amina out of the room we shared that night and tried to cry myself to sleep. But long hours after, sleep eluded me. I lifted my nightgown and examined my thighs where mere hours before, blood had come streaming down. The blood was long gone. But for the soreness and the hidden bruises on my arms, I would have sworn the...incident had never happened.

I was in so much turmoil on the inside and yet on the outside, I could not feel a thing. I had to get it out or run mad and so, I had found myself getting up to go to the bathroom where I had spotted the razor.

I picked it up without thinking, sat on the floor, lifted my nightgown again and carefully traced a short, thin line on my inner thigh out of a warped curiosity than anything else. For a second, I had felt nothing as the blood oozed out of the new wound but as the cut began to sting fiercely, I had exhaled in blessed relief.

I had traced another line, and then another, and as I gritted my teeth against the pain and watched the blood stream to the surface of the broken skin and down my thigh, I had felt vindicated. Yes, it was real. Yes, it had happened.

A trip to the doctor two months later had confirmed my mother's suspicions that I was pregnant. Pregnant at fourteen? It was not the future I would have designed for myself had I had the choice; had I been left in control. I certainly had never dreamed of a future that included being pregnant at the age of fourteen for a fifty-one-year-old man married thrice already.

"Who is the father of this baby?" Alhaji had screamed at me while my mother sobbed shamefully, and my stepmothers eyed me in disdain. "Is this why I sent you to school? To go and whore yourself around? Do you know how much shame you have brought to this family, you slut?"

I wish that I had had the courage then to spit in his eye, but I had kept mute, quivering as he lambasted me in fury.

"WHO IS THE FATHER OF THIS BABY?" He had bellowed again, his eyes bulging out of their sockets.

"Alhaji Bamaiyi." I had eventually muttered, taking a twisted pleasure in the shocked silence that followed my answer.

Once the truth had been uncovered, meetings upon meetings were held—meetings I was never invited to sit in on.

The men will handle it, Hajia had kept reassuring me. *Let's leave the rest to Allah*.

Alhaji Bamaiyi had first claimed I seduced him, then he had blamed it on the devil, and then at last, he had become ever so contrite and willing to take me back as his lawful wife despite the grievous sin I had made him commit against his body and mine.

Seven and a half months later, I had had the son that Alhaji Bamaiyi had been hoping for earnestly. My baby boy, Abu. Yes, *that* Abu. He had not exactly been bouncing, having been born prematurely but he had been healthy enough. Everyone had been so concerned with the plight of my new baby boy that no one had later remembered to ask about the crisscross of old cuts on my thighs.

I had thought I would hate Abu. Sure enough, I had resented him every day he had grown larger inside me. But from the moment I had heard his first cry, my heart had torn at the realization that he could be the one good thing that came out of this, that he was a part of me, and as angry as I was about my circumstance, there was no turning my back on my own.

At that point, Alhaji Bamaiyi had ramped up the pressure on my parents to let Abu and me move in with him but my mother, surprisingly for her, had dug her heels in and insisted that being a young mother, I needed to remain at home where she could take care of me herself for the time being.

More surprisingly, Alhaji had sided with her. He had not done so out of benevolence. Rather, his pride had been bruised by how Bamaiyi had handled things, and he had wanted to spite him and get what retribution he could by denying him direct access to his son.

In the end, Bamaiyi, not wanting to lose my father's patronage, had agreed to pay my bride price and let Abu and I remain with my father until I was through with school, at which point they would both agree on next steps. I had transferred schools to Gatesbridge where I had to repeat a year. It had turned out to be the best thing because there, I met the three best friends who had come to mean more than anyone else to me except Abu.

I had introduced Abu to everyone outside of my family as my little brother, not so much out of embarrassment but more out of a determination to put the past firmly behind me. As far as I wanted everyone to be concerned, none of it had ever happened.

But that is no longer going to be the case. Not now that Alhaji has decided to return my son and me, as though we were old baggage, to the house of the sick, sadistic monster that raped and got me pregnant at fourteen.

It is plain as day that Alhaji is doing this to punish me for my insolence. Hajia had told me about Alhaji Bamaiyi sniffing around months ago and my father had not said a word then. It is because I have continued to defy him that he has devised my returning to Bamaiyi as the fitting penalty.

I stare at my father now with hatred gleaming in my eyes.

How does he expect me to go live with the monster who ruined what should have been the carefree years of my life? How does he expect me to live with the beast who is the reason I never stop looking over my shoulder? What have I done to Allah to deserve a father who torments his daughter this way? What have I done to deserve such an ill-fated life?

"I won't go!" I force the words through the lump lodged in my throat. "I won't. And if you make me go, you'll be sorry."

He curls his mouth in contempt as he reclines fully on his daybed. "You're a woman now, not a child. You better start acting like one."

And with a wave of his hand, he dismisses me.

He knows nothing. I will not be easily dismissed this time. He and his cohort have stolen years of my life and are attempting to steal what is left without a care.

What will I tell my friends—that I am being married off to the man who raped me? The man who happens to be the father of the little boy they have always thought to be my brother?

What will I tell Dimeji—that I am not in fact the innocent he thought me, saddled as I am with a husband and a son?

What will I tell Abu—that the woman he thought to be his mother is not, and his mother is in fact the girl he has thought to be his favorite sister?

Who will be held responsible for this new season of chaos? I bore the brunt the last time. Not this time. They cannot make me, not when I am regaining some semblance of control. This time, I will not be dismissed. This time, *they* will be sorry.

CHAPTER TWENTY-FIVE
Lara

...ONE MISTAKE AND I'VE screwed up the rest of my life. Who has a direct line to Father Time? I need him to come see about restarting this bitch.

THE DIAGNOSIS WAS OFFICIAL and confirmed. Acute Hepatitis B.

Funny, the news had yet to sink in for my family. They kept staring at me like I would keel over any moment, like I had an end-stage disease or something.

I was having a hard time digesting it myself. I would convince myself that I did not look different, that I did not feel all that different, that everything was as it should be but then, I would spot the varied bottles of medications scattered on my dressing table and remember that everything was nowhere near fine.

I kept screaming out loud in my head. *I only used that needle once. I only used it that one time.*

I had come clean to Mom and Dad about shooting myself up with morphine, but I had not been able to bring myself to tell them why. Instead, I let them assume that I had been acting out as usual.

Now, all Mom had to do was look at me and break down in tears. She went around with an injured look on her face like she had no clue what she had done to be burdened with such a demon child.

If she kept it up, I could see myself breaking down and yelling at her. *This is your fault, stupid! You and the stupid James you brought into our lives, making me want to do anything, anything at all, to escape!*

I would have done anything, anything at all, to escape the memory of his arms. They had always felt wrong holding me. They had always been a tad too close for comfort.

You know I love you to the moon and back, he would whisper as he slid into my bed when Mom fell asleep. He would rub his hands over my head and kiss my cheek. And like the child I had been, I had felt loved.

You make everything fade away, the ugliness, the bitterness, everything. I could just drown in your eyes, he would tell me. And like the stupid child I had been, I had felt beautiful.

I just want to hold you, he would say. *There is nothing wrong with it. Nothing.* And like the stupid, dirty child I had been, I had felt wanted.

I had liked it at first. Liked being held, being wanted, feeling needed, believing he preferred me to Mom. James preferred me to Mom.

We must keep this between us, he would whisper. *Nobody will understand it like we do. They won't understand our connection. Nobody can. Nobody but me...and you.* And like the fool of a child I had been, I had felt like I belonged.

Before long, holding me had no longer been enough for James, of course. On a typical night, he would rub his hands over my head, kiss my cheek, and hold me. One night, he hadn't stopped there.

No, one night, he had trailed his lips from my cheek to my lips. I had drawn back in surprise and distaste, suppressing a sound of distress.

What? He laughed. *You've never been kissed before?*

I shook my head. I was ten.

Wow, he said in awe, *you're so different. You're so pure and beautiful.*

I eyed him skeptically.

Let me show you how pure and beautiful you are. Trust me.

He had reached out, lifted me up, and to my confusion and consternation, had begun to slide me up and down his lap in increasing agitation. He shuffled me around in a series of jerky motions before gasping and shuddering violently.

Disgusted, I felt something wet spread through the back of my nightgown. It was all I could do to not throw up as he held on to me tightly, trying to bring his shuddering to a gradual halt.

Trust me, he had said, *I'll show you how pure and beautiful you are.*

I had not felt beautiful. I sure as hell had not felt pure. I had felt like a fallen angel with a dirty face and soiled wings.

I don't like that. I don't want you to do that again, I told him, sure he would understand but he had pushed me away, a peculiar expression in his eyes.

That night had been the beginning of an interminable nightmare. Every night, he would come into my room and I could do nothing but cry feebly as he shuffled me up and down his lap, telling me how much he loved me.

I could not walk around the house during the day when he was home without his eyes creepily following my every step. He would not let me have friends over and if he happened to catch me talking to a guy on the phone, he would scream at my befuddled mother about how loose and uncontrollable I had become.

He never yelled at me directly, not in front of her. He would wait until she had fallen asleep before creeping to my room to give me a stern lecture about how dangerous boys were—*they just want what you've got, sweetie*—before climbing into my bed.

Sometimes, he was content with jerking me around on his lap. Other times, he would be more intrepid, touching my budding breasts, trying to get me to touch him. He kept getting brasher as time went by.

The nightmare had ended abruptly a random Sunday morning when Mom slammed the divorce papers in front of him at breakfast. Apparently, he had been having an affair with a co-worker. We were out before the day was over.

I did not know if Mom had known what James had done, had been doing to me. They had been arguing more and more—about her extended hours at work, about the unpaid bills, about some woman, about some other woman, about this and about that but if she had known about James and me, she had never said a word.

But here we were, acute Hepatitis B. The first thing I had done when I woke up this morning was gaze at my reflection in the mirror and say out loud, "I have hepatitis. Acute Hepatitis B."

I had started my intensive viral immunosuppressive medication therapy immediately my final lab results had come in. In Dr. Iroh's opinion, I was 'lucky' because they had caught the chronic infection in its early stages so my chances of beating it were remarkably high. Uh huh, what darn luck.

It would be quite the understatement to say that I found the drugs abhorrent. There was a glimmer of hope in that once the disease was suppressed, there was a good chance I could go off the drug therapy and simply have to be monitored as opposed to being treated but only time would tell. Until then, I had to swallow these numerous revolting pills and wait. Wait like a prisoner handed a death penalty, playing the waiting game with death.

Everything was fucked up right now, and I did not need anyone to excuse my French, damn it. The first third of the school year had started up without a hitch approximately four months ago. With less than a week to go before school shut down for the Christmas holidays, the term was in flipping shambles.

Aside the fact that I was likely to drop dead any second from a progressively failing liver, Fola's dad had died. He pulled a fast one on everybody and chunked the deuce. Fola had had to skip all her exams and re-schedule them for later during the holidays. She would not be returning to school until next term. Some holidays. Mourning her dad and worrying about crappy make-up exams to boot.

Something was off with Bibs as well. She had come to school yesterday so distraught that she was barely able to complete her last exam. She would not confide in Dimeji, Abi, not even me.

"Bibs, what the hell is going on with you?" I had cornered her in the bathroom during lunch.

Tears had come to her eyes almost instantaneously.

"Nothing, Lara. It's nothing. I'm tired, a little distracted."

"Why, what's distracting you so much?"

"It's not a big deal!"

"Not a big deal or you don't want to share? Which is it?"

"Why don't you tell me what's up with you?" She turned the tables around. "It's not just malaria, Lara, is it?"

I stared at her in surprise. "What do you mean?"

"Lara, you've been coming late to school some mornings straight from the hospital. You're always at the sick bay, taking one medication or the other. It does not look like malaria to me."

"So, you noticed, huh? Color me shocked seeing how wrapped up you've been in Dimeji. I can't believe that you've been able to take in anything outside of him. Have you even tried to reach out to Fola after...?" My voice had broken off.

"Lara, don't."

"Don't what? Tell you what a lousy friend you are? Tell you how you aren't there for your friends when they need you because of a guy? No, tell me what has you so distracted. You and Dimeji had a fight?"

Her eyes turned flinty. "You think you know everything, don't you?"

"What? Isn't this about Dimeji? Correct me if I am wrong."

"I'm not going to bother. I thought you would know better but please, it's you we're talking about. It's Lara, the one who thinks she has the license to say anything to anyone when and how she pleases. What gives you the right to sit on a pedestal and judge everybody else?

"Have you ever stopped to think that while you're fine judging yourself so harshly, the rest of us don't want to be held to your impossible standards? See, I keep making excuses for you being cruel and inconsiderate all the time. I tell myself that you don't know any better, but you know what? I've been lying for you!

"You are cruel, and you are hateful and even worse, you are that to us, your so-called best friends. What are you taking out on us? What has you so messed up that you try to mess everybody else up too? And now, you're turning on me? You think you know everything, don't you? You don't! Just...leave me alone!"

I had watched her departing figure in hurt, not believing that Bibs could lash out that way, and at me of all people. It had hurt more because she had said nothing but the truth. Abi had blown up at me for the same reason.

I did not know how to *not* take out my angst on the people I loved, on the people who loved me. I knew when I was doing it, I did not know how to *stop* doing it. Perpetually terror-stricken that people would love me and inevitably hurt me in the name of loving me, I figured I would hop in there and beat them to it.

I had spammed Bibs on her phone a countless number of times yesterday to apologize but she had not responded. I had even tried to reach her on her family landline but that had not worked either. Even more worrying, she had not shown up at school today.

I was jerked out of my thoughts as Abi dropped down next to me under the gum tree.

Since our fight, she and I had barely managed to be civil with each other. She had said some horrible things to me and had subsequently showed no sign of remorse whatsoever. I was surprised that she had come now to join me.

I watched as she stretched out her legs with a pensive look on her face.

"Are you alright?" I asked. She was still one of my best friends. Besides, with Fola and Bibs off the radar, it was the both of us left standing...her at least, anyway. I, on the other hand, could kick the bucket any second, no thanks to Hep B.

"Are you alright?" I asked again. She did not seem to have heard me.

She started. "What? Yes, yes, I'm...alright."

"You don't look it. Are things cool at home? With your mom?"

She appeared to think over the question before replying quietly, "Yes, home is fine. It's...everything else is crazy."

"Tell me about it!" I snickered bitterly. "This wasn't what I meant when I prayed for an exciting school year."

"Have you spoken to Bibs yet? Dimeji asked me if I had. He said he hasn't been able to get a hold of her since yesterday."

"I haven't, either. I saw Amina earlier and asked about Bibs, but she was rather vague. I'm not sure what to think."

She murmured in agreement.

I went on. "We couldn't wait for this school year to be over when it first started. I still can't wait but for the wrong reasons now. This has got to be the most horrible term ever.

"The holidays are going to be depressing too. Manny is leaving any day now, and I haven't had time to let that sink in. Fola obviously won't be in the holiday spirit, there's something strange going on with Bibs and she's mad at me, and—"

"I'm pregnant."

I spun around in shock.

She spun around too to face me, tears spilling out of her huge, usually exuberant eyes. "Lara, I'm pregnant and I don't know what the heck I am going to do!"

She began to cry as I stared at her.

"Wait, have you done a test? How do you know you are?" I asked.

"Lara, I don't understand, help me! Jimi and I used a condom every single time. The only time we didn't was the first time but like, who gets pregnant on their first time?! I was going through a grocery list for Mumsie and I realized that I hadn't seen my period in a while, but I was like whatever, it's late or something. But I bought a couple of pregnancy test kits just to... and...Lara, I'm pregnant!"

She paused for breath. "Oh my God, Lara, what am I going to do? Like, Mumsie will kill me if she finds out. What am I going to do?"

"Hang on now, do you know how far along you are?"

"About two months maybe? I've tried to calculate it but I'm too scared to go to a doctor and actually confirm."

"You might not be pregnant. I had a friend who had a pregnancy scare once and she was convinced she was pregnant until her period surprised her weeks later."

"Lara, no, trust me! I've been throwing up almost every day!"

"Holy cow! Have you told what's his name yet? Jimi?"

"Lara, this is the worst part. I feel so humiliated telling you this, but you were right! Ah my God, I've been humbled. Jimi is an asshole!"

"What do you mean? What did he do?"

"Do you want to know what he did when I told him I thought I was pregnant? Lara, Jimi beat me. This guy beat the hell out of me! Can you imagine?"

She was vibrating so hard as she told me the rest of the story that I had to grab her hands to soothe her. I hushed her as she clung onto me, trying not to show how livid I was that the ill-gotten animal had the temerity to hit her.

"He beat me and kicked me out of his house, telling me to go meet my other boyfriends who were responsible, that I was just some girl he picked off the streets! I've been calling him nonstop, but he keeps cutting off my calls! I can't believe he's doing this! How could he do this to me?"

"Don't worry about Jimi right now," I told her, doing a shoddy job of hiding my shock. "He is an asshole, fair enough, but we can worry about him later. Right now, let's focus on you and what we're going to do about...this."

"But what am I going to do, Lara? I can't have a baby! Mumsie will kill me, I swear to God. You know I'm not exaggerating. She will kill me!"

This was a heck of a situation. Abi's mother *would* kill her, there were no words to mince there. She would have her daughter sliced up and barbecued for dinner before she could get the p-word out.

"We'll figure it out, Abi." I lied in a soothing voice. "You don't worry, we're going to figure this out. Everything is going to be fine."

"That's what Jimi told me and see me now! He promised heaven and earth and... how could he do this to me, Lara? God, I should have known! I'm so stupid!"

"No, Abi! He's the stupid one! He has no right to treat you this way. He's evil! You're not to blame."

"Lara, I trusted this guy! I loved this guy! I love him! I thought he loved me too. He told me all these beautiful things and I bought them and yet, see how he treated me like he had never seen me before in his life.

"He told me he would be there for me, no matter what and now, he isn't. And I warned him to be careful with my heart. I was so scared of getting hurt and I begged him to take care of my heart and he promised he would. Now, look what he's done with it. He's broken my heart, Lara! My heart's breaking and I can't bear it!"

I shook my head imperceptibly as she continued to cry.

I had always perceived Abi to be the type who needed to fall and learn the hard way about trusting so easily. My intuition was turning out to be right but seeing her break down now, I wished she could have learned the lesson any other way but this.

I wished I did not have to sit here and hold her as the scales fell off her eyes. I wished I were not in the front row seat watching the transformation from naiveté to disillusionment.

After all, I had watched that transformation one time too many in my own damn self.

CHAPTER TWENTY-SIX
Fola

...OVER FOURTEEN DAYS since Daddy's been gone. To be candid, it doesn't feel that different, given that we never saw him that much. My chest hurts.

It is Christmas Day in two days. It won't be our first without him. He'd been away on business trips previous Christmases. I guess we know now he'd been alternating the holidays between us and...gee, my chest really hurts. Who knows if it will hurt for the rest of my life?

YOU COULD HAVE CUT the atmosphere in the room with a knife. Mommy, Sayo, and I were sitting at one end of our huge living room flanked by Aunty Folake, Uncle Dapo (Mommy's older brother) and Mommy's lawyer, Mr. Marinho.

On the other side of the room was the ugly hag with her uglier children huddled on either side of her. They had their legal representative in tow—two lawyers in a classic case of overdoing things. She had also come with three older women. Her family, friends, I couldn't care less.

Daddy's lawyer, Mr. Opia, sat in an armchair which one of the maids had moved in place ahead of his arrival. He would turn to observe one side of the room, then the other, and then he would clear his throat and return to pretending to study the papers in front of him.

His lanky assistant kept his eyes glued to the wall in front of him as though leery of being struck down by eye contact with either of the two parties on opposite sides of the room.

It was a little over two weeks since Daddy's death and here we were, gathered like hungry vultures to pick at his leftovers.

I shuffled my feet edgily. Mommy, Aunty Folake and Uncle Dapo were embroiled in a subdued conversation that I could not make out. Sayo was sitting by himself, a truculent expression on his face making it patently clear that he did not want to be engaged, talk less of approached.

I surreptitiously risked a glance at the enemy camp deep in their own subdued conversation, and I inadvertently caught the eyes of the older boy that everyone claimed looked exactly like Daddy.

When Aunty Folake arrived earlier, she had gathered me in a too-tight hug and asked how I was feeling. Her question had drawn a blank for me.

How are you feeling? How was I feeling? I did not know how I was feeling. I did not know that I was feeling at all.

Wait, that was not true. Mostly, I felt hollow. Empty.

In contrast, the bags under Mommy's eyes were heavy and full, like clouds turning dark and furious, heavy with raindrops, just before the storm let loose.

Whenever I saw those hefty bags under her bloodshot eyes, and the unshed tears in Sayo's jaded eyes, I wanted nothing more than to stomp on Daddy's corpse until he gasped back to life so I could kill him all over again.

Those times, I felt full. Full of something deep and dark. But mostly, I felt...empty.

I had secretly scorned my best friends for their crazy, not-so-perfect families but the joke was on me now—my mother, brother and I forced in the same room with this ugly cow and her calves to listen to and possibly contest my father's will.

I did not see the need for this meeting, and I did not understand why we would possibly have to contest anything in the first place. Mommy was Daddy's wife, period. I did not care what the lawyers parroted, and I did not care what papers this other she-devil had as proof. I refused to recognize her and her children as anything but usurpers.

The older boy was staring at me with no shame whatsoever. I stared him down with unconcealed hatred until he blinked and took his eyes away, the chicken. I wondered briefly if we had come as a total surprise to him as much as he and his family had come to us.

Before my thoughts could wander any further, Mr. Opia cleared his throat the loudest he had since he arrived. I judged correctly that that was his cue for the meeting to begin.

He began with a rambling spiel about the sadness and gloom that Daddy's death had left everyone in. *On behalf of Samuels and Associates, we would like to offer our heartfelt condolences, yada, yada, etc., etc.*

I stifled my yawns and tuned out as he yammered on. Sayo was restlessly fidgeting beside me. Were lawyers always this verbose? I could barely understand a word of the legalistic drivel.

I pricked my ears up as I tuned in to hear Mr. Opia say, "...two months ago, our client requested a meeting, informing us that he wanted to restructure his will."

That caught everyone's attention. I felt the air in the room crackle with new tension.

"We had had two meetings with him to review, after which he had decided, against our legal advice, to destroy all copies of his former will prior to completing a new draft. We had been in the process of working with him to draft a new will before his sudden and regrettable accident. Unfortunately, this new version of his will was not completed before his untimely demise." Mr. Opia concluded.

All the adults broke out in murmurs at the last ominous statement.

"So, what are you saying?" One of the old hag's minions queried him loudly. "That there is no will?"

"Well..." Mr. Opia cleared his throat. "As of the time of his death, Chief Adeyemi's new will was not completed. We were in the preliminary stages of re-assessing the value of the assets and property making up his estate but the actual will was yet to be formalized and put into writing."

"What happens now?" Uncle Dayo asked briskly.

"What do you mean what happens now?" The old hag barked loudly in Yoruba. It was the first time she had addressed our side of the room since she arrived with her underlings.

"What do you mean? If there is no will, then everything will go to his oldest child and first son, Bidemi. He will then decide how everything should be split and distributed. That is the way things are done."

A terrible silence followed her words.

His oldest child?

"That's the way things are done where?" Aunty Folake asked incredulously.

"Madam, why don't we let Mr. Opia finish what he is saying?" Uncle Dayo said coldly to the hag who eyeballed him like she had sprouted a demonic horn and wanted nothing more to gore him.

She ignored him and said again, "That's how things are done where we are from. In the absence of a will, everything goes to the first child."

I waited impatiently for Mommy to speak up, but she remained dumb. I observed her in increasing irritation. Mommy had always been the laid-back, easy-going type, not given to hysterics, willing to sit down and resolve conflict peacefully but she had never been without a backbone either.

Since the truth about Daddy came out, she had tapped out and become unnervingly complacent about everything, like she did not care anymore. Case in point, this she-devil was craftily trying to bully us out of what was rightfully ours and Mommy had yet to say a word, to stand up for us for once. I was not having it.

"I don't think you know what you are talking about but FYI, I am his first child!" I spoke up in a loud and defiant tone.

Every eye in the room turned to ogle me in shock. No one seemed to know what to say next.

Aunty Folake cleared her throat then. "I think the children should be excused before we deliberate any further on this matter."

Mr. Opia hurriedly agreed. "That would be a good idea."

I opened my mouth to disagree, but Mommy chose to recover her voice at last. "Fola, Sayo, why don't you show Bidemi and Bisoye to the other living room?" she asked, her voice barely audible in the subtle rancor that had enveloped the room.

I glanced at Mommy in surprised annoyance, and the she-devil pursed her mouth like she had been forced to suck on a rotting lemon before she nodded at her boys to follow us.

I reluctantly led the way to the other living room, followed closely by the demon spawns. Sayo chose instead to go upstairs to his room without a word.

I curled up in one of the armchairs and closed my eyes, reopening them almost instantly when I felt movement beside me. Bidemi was settling into the armchair next to me. Bisoye, much more timid, had taken a place on the edge of the sofa farther away.

I chanced a glance at Bidemi and before I could look away, he caught my eye.

"This is some crazy business, huh?" He half-smiled hesitantly.

I looked away pointedly.

He did not take the hint. "I'm sorry for...your loss."

"I'm sure you are!" I said in a strangled tone, simmering over his audacity.

"He was my father too—"

"You don't say!"

"—and I would never have thought that he could have done something like this."

I looked at him then.

He snickered wryly. "Does it surprise you to hear me admit that? I'd always thought him shady. In retrospect, we should have known. Deep inside, I'm sure we did. He was always on the road—Milan, Dallas, Hong Kong, Canada, everywhere, anywhere but home. As far I can remember, he was never home."

He stopped, outwardly abashed at having revealed so much but his words having created a startling, tenuous bridge between us for the time being.

I glanced over to where Bisoye was perched, hunched over and seemingly ready to take flight at the slightest provocation. He was so small. He could not have been more than ten, eleven at most.

"Do you want anything to drink, Bisoye?" I found myself asking.

He started in surprise as though he could not believe I was addressing him.

"N-n-no. No, thank you," he said shyly, his eyes barely meeting mine.

We flinched as loud, arguing voices filtered in from the other living room.

"They sound like they are going at it in there," Bidemi said.

I nodded.

"If only there was a way to turn back time so we weren't here, man."

I had to disagree.

"I don't!" I bit out vehemently. "I prefer to know him for who he really is...was. I'd rather that than live the rest of my life painting this picture of a hero who never was."

"I have to give to him, he pulled this off for a while. I wonder how much longer he thought he could have fooled everyone."

"I'm sure he thought he had much longer than he did."

"He thought wrong," Bidemi said. A couple of seconds later, he mumbled, "I never liked the man, you know."

"I know what you mean. I loved him but I'm not sure I liked him too."

We exchanged tentative, rueful smiles.

Later, when the meeting had ended and everyone had left, I went downstairs to the living room to find the novel I'd been buried in before our unwelcome visitors had arrived.

The living room was dark, but I could make out the shadow of someone sitting alone in the corner.

"Mommy?"

She turned around, startled. "Oh, it's you, Fola. Is everything alright?"

I walked over to her side. "How did the rest of the meeting go?"

"Ah, it went." She breathed out heavily. "I'm so tired. There is so much to do."

"Like what and what?"

"We have to plan the funeral, you know, pick a date that works for everyone. We have to have some more meetings to tidy up your daddy's estate, clean up the loose ends and—"

"How about the will?" I interrupted her. "What's going to happen with that?"

"Ah, the almighty will." She tutted. "It's like Mr. Opia said, your daddy never finished rewriting his new will and in a situation like this where we have to deal with a...third party, it's going to become a long, protracted battle that I'm not sure I'm ready to put us through."

"Does that mean you're going to let them take anything, everything?"

"Not everything. We will be keeping this house. Your dad also had separate accounts and properties in my name, so we'll be okay in the end, no need to fret. We don't need to fight for anything."

"Why won't you fight? Why are you giving up so easily?" I asked agitatedly. I found it hard to swallow that she would give up without trying.

"Fight for what, Fola?" Her voice was dull with fatigue. "For what? The properties? The money? We'll end up in court for years and years, and the only ones winning at the end of the day are the lawyers. Getting them to agree to hold today's meeting here alone took so much. I don't have the energy, and I just want this madness to be over as soon as possible. I don't want anything more to do with this. I don't want this to take any more from us than it already has, Fola. I want you, Sayo and I to move on as quickly as we can and focus on healing and living our lives."

"You're saying there's nothing worth fighting for?"

"He's gone so I don't know that there's much else left worth fighting for. Not now, not anymore," she admitted sadly as she lifted her hand to caress my cheek.

"So that evil woman wins?

"Wins what, Fola? Nobody is winning anything here. We have all lost someone that was dear to us. I wouldn't call that winning."

I chewed on that before she added, "Besides, they only win if we let this take any more from us than it already has but I am determined that we put it all behind us and move on. That's the way we win."

In that moment, I saw my mother for who she was, and not through the filter I had insisted on viewing her. She was a woman going through the fire, having lost her husband and the father of her children, the same man she had discovered had lied to her for over twenty-two years of their marriage. It was a brutal, double blow and yet, here she was taking the highway as much as it was costing her to do so.

She was willing to pay the price to ensure that this did not break both her and us, her children, and that price was walking away. She could easily choose to fight for Daddy's estate, fight to establish herself as his legally recognized wife, fight to have the final word, but she was choosing instead to walk away.

All this time, I had assumed she was backing down, walking away because she was weak and afraid, but I was wrong. What I had mistaken for impotence was power.

I felt a blend of emotions run through me—pride and shame. I was proud of Mommy, proud of her strength, proud of her forbearance, proud of her grace, and I was ashamed of myself for not being as strong, for not being as selfless.

Mommy and I had never been close. She had always been just my mother, not my friend. So, it was with some awkwardness that I asked, "Mommy, if he hadn't...died, would you...would you have left him?"

She glanced at me sharply. "Why?"

"I don't know. I'm...curious."

"Hmm, I don't know, my dear. Maybe? I don't know."

We sat in the dark a while longer and then, she confessed. "I might have asked him to leave her but...I don't know that she would have let him."

"I still can't believe that Daddy did something like this, that he did this to us!" I lamented. "How could he? Why did he? Like, I don't understand!"

She sniffed, her own eyes glistening with unshed tears.

"I hate him, Mommy!" I sobbed. "I hate him so much b-but I just... I just want him back!'

"Me too, Fola," she said as she took me in her arms. "Me too!"

I felt an intense surge of love and protection for my mother as she held me and we both wept. I had been selfish long enough, thinking only of the effect this situation had had on me. I had spared less thought for Mommy.

Never again. Right there and then, I made myself a vow that I would do anything to never see her hurt this way again.

CHAPTER TWENTY-SEVEN
Bibs

...GONE UP IN FLAMES AND barely breathing - Lebiba Gana, a self-portrait.

I HAVE BEEN IN THIS forsaken place for six hellish days. Yes, I have been counting. I have not budged an inch from this room since I moved in, not to eat or fetch myself a drink. It is not my room. It is not my home.

After my last exam, Alhaji had sent word through Hajia that I was to be prepared to leave home before the end of the year. Having played his joker, he could not stomach the sight of me long enough to tell me himself.

Bamaiyi had 'graciously' given me permission to spend the Sallah holiday with my family before I moved into his household with Abu in tow. Needless to say, that period of respite had been miserable.

Even the arrival of my favorite aunt, my mother's younger sister, had not been enough to dispel the cloud of gloom hovering over me. I had not seen my Aunt 'Mina in a long time—almost two years. And yet, I was barely able to manage a smile, much less keep up a jovial conversation with her for the duration of her stay.

I kept waiting for a last-minute miracle. I kept waiting for Alhaji to summon me to his sacred sanctum and tell me that I would not be going anywhere after all, that it had been a ploy to put me in my place by scaring me the living daylights out of me. I could have lived with that as cruel as it would have been.

No miracle had turned up for me. My things had been moved to my new home by the time Sallah was over and the last of the roasted ram had been inhaled.

I have refused to speak to anyone of my friends or Dimeji since, having turned my phone off to avoid the torment of their back-to-back calls. What would I say? *Hey, guys! Guess who has been relegated to the life of a full-fledged housewife number four at the grand, old age of eighteen!*

You heard right—no more school for me. On Alhaji's recommendation, Alhaji Bamaiyi will not let me return to school to complete my final year of A-Levels. There would be no university for me either. As though I were some village child-bride, and not an educated girl with educated parents.

I sit up now as Bamaiyi's third wife, Hadiza knocks softly on my door before pushing it open. Having just showered, I am dressed for yet another long day of reclining in bed, twiddling my thumbs, and pretending this is not my new reality.

"Will you come down for breakfast?" she asks, with a hesitant smile on her face. She is not much older than I am—twenty-two at most.

"I'm not hungry," I reply shortly. I had briefly considered a hunger fast when I first arrived but by the second evening, I had given in to the hunger pangs and allowed a maid to bring a tray to my room for each meal.

"Are you sure?" Hadiza asks again.

I ignore her this time.

Alhaja, Bamaiyi's first wife, joins her at the door. Short, rotund and dripping with pearls, Alhaja is older than her husband. She had first been betrothed to his older brother who had died in a car accident before the marriage was consummated. She had then married Bamaiyi who had wasted no time in marrying his second wife months later.

"Are you coming down for breakfast?" she addresses me.

"She said she's not hungry," Hadiza answers for me.

"I'm not hungry." I echo Hadiza.

"If she's not hungry, then she's not hungry. She's not a small girl. Get up, Lebiba, our husband wants to see you downstairs," Alhaja says in her stringent tone.

Your husband, I think as I rise slowly. *Not mine. He will never be mine, no matter what you say.*

My stomach cramping with nerves, I go down to the living room where Bamaiyi is waiting. I have not seen him since my first night here as he left for an impromptu business trip the next day. Before then, I had not seen him in years.

"Sit down." He smiles at me as I trudge in, staring at the floor.

I do so, taking care to place myself as far away from him as possible.

"How are you?" he asks in a kind tone. "Alhaja told me you haven't been eating."

I don't answer. I feel him shift and move to sit next to me. I suppress a shudder of repulsion as he lifts his hand to stroke my hair twisted in its braid as usual.

"You shouldn't have your hair in a braid anymore," he says. "You're a woman now. You're a wife. My wife."

I am unable to suppress the shudder then.

"Are you cold?"

I turn away under the guise of shaking my head.

"I want you to be happy. I want you to be as happy as you and our son have made me. If you need anything, anything at all, all you have to do is ask."

"Will you let me go back to school?" I ask on a whim.

He leans back and studies me critically. "Why are you so eager to go back to school? Everything you need is here in your new home. Your husband and your son, and you will have more sons to take care of. There will be no time for school, you'll see."

"Please let me go back to school."

"Do you have a lover waiting for you there?" he asks.

Maybe if I tell him I do, he will return me to Alhaji as used goods. "I have hundreds."

He stops stroking my hair and chuckles. "Don't talk like a child, my dear. It doesn't become you."

"But I am a child next to you. Why don't you let me go?"

His tone changes then. "Don't be a silly girl."

My mother comes over later to see me and check on Abu who, like me, is not taking to the transition too well.

I do not know why she bothers as I have had my fill of her forlorn face during my last week at home. Having her around here makes me more miserable if that is possible.

A mother is supposed to be a lioness, you see, fighting for the best for her children. Hajia has never fought for me, all she does is give up. That is all she has done since she gave her life to Alhaji. It is one thing to give up on herself, it is entirely another to give up on her children. The latter is unforgivable to me.

She was not there when the damage was done. She was not there *after* the damage was done. She was not there then, and I do not need her here now.

"Alhaja says you're not eating." She fusses at me. She has already fed Abu and put him down to nap. I pay her no attention.

"Lebiba, I know this is not ideal, but we have to make the best of the situation."

I blow up at her. "Who is 'we'? Tell me! Who is 'we'? I'm the one here, not you. I'm the one here forced to make the best out of this impossible situation! All you've managed to do is be as useless as a wet rag!"

"Stop shouting, Lebiba!" Hajia cries. "Do you want everyone in the house to hear you? What is wrong with you?"

"What is wrong with *me*? How can you look at me, Hajia, and ask me that question? Look around you, is this where I should be? I should be with my friends, enjoying the holidays. I shouldn't be here playing wife to a man who raped me when I was fourteen!"

"Lebiba, don't say things like that!"

"Hajia, stop it! Just stop! What is wrong with *you*? You don't get to hide your face from the truth. Who are you to be in denial if I am not in denial? He raped me, Hajia. Raped! He raped me before I had breasts! Yet you let Alhaji send me back to him. Are you sure you gave birth to me? How could you let them bring Abu and I back here? Hajia, how?"

"Calm down!" She cries, tears filling her eyes.

"Don't tell me to calm down! I've been calm long enough! If you people want to kill me, why don't you kill me already? What did I do to deserve all of this? You won't be happy until I am dead?"

"What can I do?" She sobs.

"Don't ask me that! You're the mother, not me! Get me out of here, Hajia! Get me out of here, please, before I go mad!"

"Lebiba..."

"Don't you understand, Hajia? I want...I want to go home!" I fling myself on my bed and break down for the first time since I arrived in hell.

I disregard Hajia's pathetic pleadings until she gives up and leaves. As she does, I swim in my emergency reservoir of tears until I drift off to sleep.

The sound of a key turning in the lock rouses me. I look up to see Bamaiyi standing at the foot of my bed, and I swallow hard. It is the first time he has stepped into my room after I moved in. It could only mean one thing. I glance at the clock. It is already ten o'clock.

"Are you alright?" he asks gravely. "Alhaja said you were throwing a tantrum earlier."

I start sobbing again. "I want to go home. Let me go home."

He sits beside me and takes my hand. "My wife, I told you I will take care of you. There is no need for you to cry. This is home. You're home."

I am shivering now.

"You're so beautiful. Stop crying. I don't like to see you cry. I want to make you happy."

"Please..." I whimper uselessly.

He kisses the side of my forehead. I flinch and head for the door. He rises in surprise and pulls me back. I push away from him as hard as I can, and he pulls at me again, roughly this time.

"What do you think you're doing?" he asks fiercely. "Where do you think you're going?"

I push hard against him again and this time, he shakes me. Hard. I aim a blow at his nose in retaliation which he counters by twisting my arm behind me. Suddenly, I am fighting like an enraged, hostile demon separated from a captive soul, but I quickly discover that I am no match for his aroused strength.

Not again, please. Not again.

I struggle to no avail, biting at his hands as he pushes me onto the bed face down, using his arms and knees to restrain me before reaching to roughly pull up my skirt, leaving my lower back exposed to his gaze. What in the name of God is he doing?

I twist backwards to see his face, but his grip on me is tight. I kick out with my legs, hoping to hit him in the groin, and get a smart blow across the head for my efforts.

I give up then. It is no use postponing the inevitable. My body sags, and tears well up in my eyes as I stop fighting.

Dimeji.

I start to bawl at the unwelcome invasion, at the violation of the memories of the gentle and beautiful handprints left on my body by the one I have willingly given myself to, at the violation of those memories by these familiar yet still unwelcome hands.

Dimeji, I fought.

I weep bitterly as I bite down on the pillow underneath my head and detach myself from what is happening behind me.

The beast does not let me go when he is done. Slick with sweat, he shifts over and strokes my head as I stare into space, tears trickling unbidden from my eyes.

"You shouldn't fight me. I'm your husband." He wipes my eyes tenderly. "If you fight me, it'll hurt you and I don't want to hurt you. You'll get used to it; you'll see. Just don't fight me."

I do not respond to his soft entreaties. I lie there, motionless, like a broken doll, broken in every sense of the word.

When he is through trying to get a response from me, he leaves my room gloomily. I run into the bathroom, barely making it in time to throw up in the toilet bowl. After retching and emptying my stomach, I sink to the floor, howling. My tears are in limitless supply.

This is to be my life now. Fending off the approach of a rapist husband night after night after night? Playing possum while he makes me relive the nightmares day after day after day?

There is no way I can go on like this, you see. If this is all that I have to look forward to for the rest of my life, I am ready to give it up. Yes, I am ready to give up the rest of my life. They can have it along with everything else they have taken from me.

CHAPTER TWENTY-EIGHT
Abi

...LEFT MUMSIE AND I TO live in England, I had been heartbroken, or I'd thought I was.

I would wait eagerly for his calls every other weekend when he would tell me how much he missed me and how he couldn't wait for me to join him when he was settled.

But then, he had remarried, and the weekend calls had come through with much less frequency. He wasn't so sure anymore when I could come over to join him. I had been heartbroken, or I'd thought I was.

Then he had had another child, and the weekend calls had come once in a blue moon. His newly expanded family meant there was no space left for me to come over and in time, Popsie became a stranger to me. I had been heartbroken, or I'd thought I was.

But then, Jimi. Jimi, the square peg I tried to fit into the gaping hole that was Popsie.

My father hadn't broken my heart all this time, I realize now. He had only chipped away at it little by little.

But then, Jimi. Jimi, who with one strike, smashed what was left to smithereens. Now I know the true definition of a heartbreak.

NOTHING HAD CHANGED. I was still pregnant. I prayed fervently every day. I had even taken things up a notch and fasted this week but alas, I was still pregnant.

Christmas was long gone. Mumsie and I planned to attend church later tonight for the 'watch-night' service when she returned from work. According to her, there was nothing like ringing in a new year with the Lord. With a bit of luck, I would be ringing in the new year with a fresh start and without a *you-know-what*. Fingers crossed.

To date, the people in the know about this...thing remained Jimi, Lara, and Tracy, my neighbor.

Tracy had beat me to the telling. The smell of the fried fish Mumsie had had for dinner one night had set off the now familiar but still awful nausea. Gripped with fear, I had dashed outside to throw up surreptitiously and as I washed out my mouth and my face with water from the borehole tap, Tracy had come up to me.

"Hmm, Abi, are you pregnant?" she asked. I tried to look at her, fear churning away in my belly but found myself turning away to throw up some more.

Finally, the nausea had subsided, and I had asked, "how...how did you know?"

"Been there, done that." She had given me a coy look and flashed her pearly whites. "Twice."

I stared at her.

"Do you know what you're going to do about it?" she asked.

I shook my head in reply.

"What did you do?" I wanted to know.

"Are you sure you want to know?" She had smiled coyly again. Mumsie had ordered me in before I could reply. Since then, Tracy and Lara had become my confidants. Jimi, not so much.

For a while there, I had been convinced that Jimi would come around, that he would call to beg me and apologize, telling me that he had never meant to treat me the way he had, and that he had over-reacted out of shock but that had never happened.

I had called him the day after my exams, most of which I had performed horribly in, were over. I had screwed up my courage, dialed his number and to my surprise, a lady had picked up.

"H-Hello?" I said uncertainly.

"Who is this?" she asked curtly.

"Um... can I speak to Jimi?"

"Jimi is not here."

"Who is this?" I had asked.

"I'm Jimi's fiancée. Who are you?"

I had dropped the phone in disbelief. Jimi's *what*?

Perplexed, I redialed his number. This time, he had picked up.

"Abi, didn't I tell you not to call me again?"

"Jimi, who picked up when I called before?"

"That was my fiancée."

"Your what? Jimi, you have a fiancée? You never told me you were engaged? How did...?"

"Don't ever call this number again," he said coldly. "Goodbye."

Click. Dial tone.

Shellshocked and desperate, I had taken an Uber over to his place a couple days later.

His gateman easily recognized me. "Ah, Aunty Abi, longest time *o*!" He crowed.

"Long time. Is your *oga* around?"

"Mr. Jimi no dey house."

"Do you know when he'll be back?"

Suddenly, he couldn't look at me. "I no know *o*! *Im* comot house now with Madam."

"Madam?" I repeated stupidly.

"*Ehn*, that is, yes. Madam done come back from abroad. It done reach maybe like two weeks now. Before now, she no waka come this side for almost one year *o*, but e be like say she done full ground now."

I had thanked him and left but not before warning him not to tell Jimi that I had stopped by.

Getting home, I had broken down, baffled and desolated to learn that Jimi had had a fiancée all the while. This man had really set out to ruthlessly deceive and use me. I had sent him a text the next day full of manic curses. He never replied, and I had not heard from him since. No plot twist there.

It was a solemn Christmas for me. I could only be thankful that Mumsie had not noticed my episodes of nausea. Then again, she was almost never at home. Even Christmas Day had been a bust because she had had to work over-time.

Unlike our relatives, Mumsie and I never traveled to the East during the holidays to see her parents. They had disowned her when she married Popsie, refusing to accept him because he was not Igbo. She had been estranged from them as a result and her subsequent divorce had not helped matters.

Popsie had mailed me a box of chocolates as usual for Christmas which I had tossed in the bin. He had not bothered to call. Some father he was. I was done making excuses for him. I was done with men, period. They were only good for loving and leaving you when you needed them the most.

Christmas had been a bust for my friends too with Fola in mourning for her father, Bibs absolutely nowhere to be found, and Lara struggling with her health.

Lara had been diligent about calling to check up on me almost every day.

"So, have you agreed to visit the doctor's now? Abi, you know you need to have proper tests done." She had argued when we spoke yesterday.

"Where am I going to find a doctor? I can't go to the hospital Mumsie and I are registered at because they will reach out to her, and there is no way in hell that I can let Mumsie find out about this. She will kill me!"

"At some point, you're going to have to tell her. You can't do this by yourself!"

"I can't tell her! There's no way I can! It's not possible."

"How about your dad? Can he maybe talk to her?"

I laughed scathingly. "As if. He can't even talk to me. He didn't even call me on Christmas Day!"

"Do you want to talk to my mom? She could maybe talk to yours or something."

"Lara, I appreciate it, but I can't bring Mumsie into this. I might as well dig my grave and go lie in it if I do that. Can you just imagine how she will react?"

"So, what are you going to do? You're going to keep quiet and pretend this baby doesn't exist until it pops out while you're having a poop?"

I giggled at the image. It was the first time in days I had had a good laugh.

"You're a joker!" I told her.

"I'm glad I made you laugh but..."

"Let's talk about you, Lara. What's going on with you? It's not malaria, is it?" I confronted her.

She sighed. "You got me. No, it's not malaria. I've got Hep B."

"You have what?"

"Yeah, that was my first reaction too."

I listened as she revealed the details of her diagnosis, sensing there was more she was not saying but wise enough to leave it at that.

"Wow!" I exclaimed as she paused for breath. "This is crazy. I'm so sorry to hear this but I'm happy they caught it before it got much worse!"

"Right?"

"Is the medication working?"

"So far, so good. The prognosis is looking good too. The medication has the worst side-effects though. I feel sick and exhausted all the time, but I've got to suck it up. Once the medication quashes the virus, I shouldn't have to worry about it as much."

"Wow!"

"Wow is right. It's been tough, I won't lie. You never think about how the things you do at one point in your life can come back to haunt you later when you least expect it!"

"Tell me about it. I'm pregnant!"

We had both laughed at that.

After that conversation with Lara, I had met up with Tracy. That was when she had given me the bottle. I had unscrewed the top, taken a whiff, and almost thrown up on the spot.

"It smells like rotting eggs, right?" She cackled.

"For God's sake! What is this?" I cried.

"Don't worry. You'll hold your nose and swallow it in one go!"

I perused the bottle skeptically.

"My dear, I promised I'd help you take care of this thing," she said. "Trust me. I've done this before. You'll drink it, slip on a pad and within an hour, you'll bleed out into the pad. It'll be like having your period with cramps for one day. Before you know it, this problem will be taken care of and you won't have to worry about it again. Finito!"

"Tracy, I don't know..."

"You don't know what?"

"I don't know if I should do this. I'm not..."

"Abi, wake up!" She had said sharply. "Wake up! Are you a baby? What other option do you have? You want to have a fatherless baby, or do you think that guy is going to man up any time soon and claim you? How are you going to take care of a baby? Your mother is not going to help you out, you know that, and an abortion will be too dangerous. You could lose your life!"

"But—"

"I've told you that this is a mixture of herbs that will help your uterus contract and push everything out, simple. It's a traditional antidote. It makes your body think you're on your period, that's all. I've done this before. By the time I woke up the next day, it was like nothing ever happened."

"It won't hurt?"

"It will hurt as much as your period does on the regular. You don't want to have an actual abortion, trust me! That will be even more painful, and it is more dangerous with the quacks out there."

In the end, I had taken the little bottle from her.

I reached out now to where I had placed the bottle on my dresser last night. If anything was a walking ad for something that shouldn't be ingested, it was the content of this bottle. The liquid inside stunk like a putrefied dead rat, I swear to God.

But Tracy was right—I did not have any other viable choice. I was in no way ready to have a baby, period. Who would pay the medical costs? Who would take care of the baby and its living costs?

I would not be able to go back to school, talk less of university. Mumsie would undoubtedly abandon me in the village, after first beating me to within an inch of my life, of course. I could totally see it now.

A medical abortion was out of the question. It seemed too risky and terrifying. I was not able to fund it either and I was not going to burden my friends unduly by asking them to sort me out financially.

Be that as it may, I was not prepared to live the rest of my life burdened by something I did not want. I was not ready to spend the rest of my life paying for a stupid mistake while Jimi got off scot-free. Tracy's option, without a doubt, seemed like the safest and easiest choice.

I opened the bottle and struggled to gulp down the odious liquid, barely keeping it down. Tracy had warned me not to throw the abortifacient back up so as not to render it useless.

I ran to the kitchen and gulped down some water to get rid of the rancid aftertaste in my mouth. Next, I went to the bathroom and slipped on a sanitary pad as Tracy had instructed. Grimly, I sank down on my bed to wait. If there was a God on my side, this nightmare would be over once and for all by the end of the day.

I woke up an hour later to a biting sensation in my belly, what felt like a million bees stinging me on the inside. I managed to stagger to the bathroom where I discovered that the sanitary pad was soaked through.

Trying not to gag, I changed the pad, troubled by the amount of blood gushing out. Back in the bedroom, I discovered to my distress that I had bled so much that the blood had soaked right through my bedsheets.

I scrambled in panic to strip the bed but felt light-headed, like the strength was leaking right out of me along with the blood. I slumped on the bed to recoup my breath, the biting pain inside increasing in pressure. I clutched at my stomach, tossing from one side to another in search of relief.

Yet the pain would not ease. It was indescribable agony, liquid fire trickling through my veins. I reached down and squeezed my thigh tightly, only to lift my palm and see it covered in a dark, sticky liquid. Blood.

Scared now, I sat up to stare at the blood streaming down my ankles, and the effort to do so left me dazed.

In the distance, I heard the front door open and close. Mumsie was back.

"Abi!" She called out from the living room.

I bit back a loud moan, doubled over in pain and unable to respond.

"Abi!" She cried again. I heard her walk down to the door of my room and knock loudly. When I did not respond, she yanked at the door handle, but I had locked the door behind me prior to embarking on this idiocy.

"Abi! Are you there?" She banged on the door again.

"God! God, please!" I whimpered as I rolled off my bed, clawing at my stomach ferociously as though I could somehow strangle the pain to death.

"Abi?" She pushed against the door this time.

I half-crawled to the bathroom, thinking foolishly to get something to clean up the blood before she could see it. God, it was everywhere...on the bed, on the floor, on the wall I was propped against for support...

I never made it to the bathroom. My ankles buckled and I plummeted to the floor of my bedroom, gasping heavily for air.

Mumsie finally forced my door open and barged in.

"*Obara* Jesus!" I heard her scream and plead the blood of Jesus.

There and then, I thankfully lost consciousness and went into the void.

CHAPTER TWENTY-NINE
Lara

...THAT SHAMEFUL SECRETS take their time to grow on the inside of you like parasites, biding their time.

You're hardly aware of them until you look down one day and are taken by surprise, like an expecting mother, by the little bump you don't remember seeing the day before.

You layer up so no one sees, and while you fool people sometimes, you can't fool yourself all the time. You ignore your secrets while they grow fat on your denial.

You feel the birth pangs as the secrets roar their way to freedom. You struggle to hold them in but having laid dormant for so long, they will pay you no heed. They will exhaust your will until you give in and let them go.

So, you let go and the secrets are out. And once the secrets are out, they are no longer your own. Do you see it now? We have let go and our secrets are no longer our own.

I JUMPED UP AND RAN to envelop Fola in a gigantic hug when she strolled into the waiting room. We had only seen each other once since her father passed away. We had spoken a couple of times over the phone and even then, we had not caught up in detail as she and her family had been busy with funeral plans for her father.

"Happy New Year, love! I can't believe how long it's been since I last saw you!" I exclaimed after we let each other go.

"Happy New Year! I've missed you! I've missed all of you!"

"Same here!"

"How is she? Have you seen her yet?"

"Not yet. A nurse just came out to say that we'll be able to go in and see her any minute now."

"Wow!" Fola exclaimed as we both took our seats in the waiting room.

"Yeah." I puffed out a tired breath.

"Did you know she was pregnant? She didn't tell anyone, did she?" Fola asked.

"Um, confession time, she did tell me in confidence. I didn't know though that she had planned to do anything this insane. The last time we spoke, we were going back and forth about her options. I'd tried to get her to tell her mom, but she wasn't having it, so I let it be because I didn't want to pressure her or anything. I was blown away when her mom called to say that she was in the hospital!"

Abi and I had spoken almost every day leading up to the New Year. However, she had never mentioned a word about Tracy giving her an herbal abortifacient. She hadn't even told me that Tracy had been in the loop about her pregnancy.

Imagine my horror when a couple days after New Year's Day, I had received a call from her mother about her admission to the hospital after trying to abort the pregnancy. Yikes.

That had been one awkward conversation. Having a friend's mom ask you if you had been aware of her daughter's pregnancy and her attempt to get rid of it was not exactly my idea of a nice time.

"Why didn't she tell me?" Her mother had asked worriedly. It was the softest I had heard Abi's mother. She sounded overwrought, to say the least.

I had called Fola and Bibs afterwards to give them the news. Still unable to get a hold of Bibs, Fola and I had decided to go ahead and visit Abi in the meantime.

"Did Bibs call you back?" Fola's question hijacked my train of thought.

"I have no idea what is up with Bibs. She has been off the radar even before school let out for the holidays. It's so frustrating. Dimeji keeps pinging me all the time because he can't reach her either. Her dad must be ultra-mad at her."

"I wonder what this is about, and I hope she's okay."

"She had better be! There's too much going on around here already for her not to be!"

"I'm with you on that!" Fola agreed.

I studied her critically. She seemed the same and yet, there was something different I could not place my finger on.

"How have you been?" I asked softly.

She whistled. "Whew, that's a loaded question!"

"I know, I know, but how are you holding up? Your mom? Sayo?"

"It's been crazy, Lara. Sometimes I get up in the morning and am like...this isn't happening, but it is. It is happening and we have to...deal with it. Christmas should have been Christmas and there we were, haggling over Daddy's stuff like we were on a field trip to some market in the underworld! Ugh, it was the worst Christmas ever."

I took her hand, wincing at the hurt in her words.

"It'd have been easier if we didn't have to deal with that stupid woman!" She continued. "But we do. I mean, we did but Mommy is done. She doesn't want anything to do with any of it again. She's made up her mind that once the funeral is over, she's going to tell her lawyers to give them whatever it is they want. We're moving out of that house and selling it off. We're just going...to move on."

I nodded quietly.

"At first, I was angry, you know." The tears were glistening in her eyes now. "I couldn't believe it. This was someone that we thought we knew. This was Mommy's husband, my father and Sayo's, and we didn't know him at all.

"It's the scariest thing I've experienced. And what makes it worse is he's not here to face the music. I feel horrible saying this, but he got to die and not have to deal with the fallout. We have to. We got the short end of the stick and I kind of hate him for that."

I felt my own eyes watering. I could relate, if only a bit, how it felt to hate someone you loved, you thought you loved. *James.*

She wiped her eyes furiously. "If I can't trust my own father, who the hell can I trust? You know, whenever you guys would call me out on being self-centered sometimes, I assumed you were jealous. But I have my daddy to thank now for making me understand why you guys kept calling me out.

"If he hadn't been so selfish and self-absorbed, he would have thought about what this would do to his wife and to his children. He would have thought about us, but it is clear he never did.

"All the freaking money in the world that he made was never going to change the fact that at the end of the day, all he cared about was his freaking self and you can see the ruins he's made of us with that selfishness. Mommy couldn't get out of bed for three days running at one point!

"Sayo won't share how he truly feels with anyone. And me? I'm an emotional wreck. All because of his selfishness! So, thank you, Daddy, for that stupid lesson because I get it now. It's just too bad you had to die for me to do so!"

We stared at each other after her emotional tirade and burst into uncontrollable, frenzied laughter.

"You're going to be fine," I told her firmly once we regained control.

"I am," she replied as firmly. "That's about the only thing I am sure of."

I realized then what it was that was different about her. It was the determined and hard look in her eyes. Fola had grown up at last, albeit in a heck of a hard way.

A nurse walked up to us then. "Are you here for Miss Omonitie? You can come in and see her now."

We arose and followed the nurse down the corridor. My heart was in my throat. Ever since my diagnosis and the subsequent ongoing medication therapy, I had developed an acute fear of hospitals and the bad news held therein.

The nurse pointed out the room and we walked in hesitantly to see Abi in a hospital gown, propped up against her pillows and watching TV.

Fola and I sighed with relief and we rushed to her bedside where the three of us promptly began a concerto of tears.

"Don't you ever, ever, ever scare us like that again!" I stopped to scold Abi midway through our crying bout.

"How are you feeling?" Fola asked her.

"A little sore," Abi answered weakly. "The doctor said I lost a lot of blood and my stomach is tender. I lost my...the baby. I'm sure you know that already but...yes, I'm much better. They're discharging me tomorrow."

"Thank goodness!" Fola said as she took a seat. "I was scared to death when Lara called to tell me what had happened."

"I'm sorry for scaring everyone. Where is Bibs?"

"Hmm, Bibs has disappeared!" Fola answered.

"Ah-ah, she hasn't gotten in touch? Even now?"

"Nope!" I answered this time. "We have no idea what's going on with her."

"I hope there's nothing wrong but I'm glad you guys are here anyway."

"Where is your mom? Is she fine with...?" I trailed off, not knowing how to ask.

"As fine as she could possibly be, considering she walked in on her daughter stupidly trying to abort a baby herself like a dunce."

I smiled at her self-deprecating tone.

"I don't know what I was thinking, guys!" She cried out. "Like, I was so desperate, and I wasn't thinking straight. I could have died!"

"Have you spoken to Jimi?" I asked tentatively.

"Spoken to who?" She huffed bitterly. "What's there to talk about? 'Jimi, by the way, I was trying to abort our baby and now, I'm in the hospital, just thought you should know, have a nice day?' I don't ever want to see that bastard again!"

"Lara filled me in on this dude. How come you never told us about him?" Fola asked. "Why did you hide him from us?"

Abi exhaled nervously. "To be honest, I knew you guys wouldn't approve of him, and when I found out I was pregnant and he showed me his true colors, I was so...embarrassed."

She sniveled quietly, and Fola and I got up from our chairs to console her.

"You have nothing to be embarrassed about, Abi," I told her. "You fell in love with the wrong guy. It happens to the best of us."

"No, falling in love doesn't excuse my being stupid!" She protested. "I knew there was something off right from the moment I met him. And you cautioned me, Lara! But I chose to ignore my gut because I was flattered that he was interested in me. He made me do things I didn't want to, and I always gave in because I didn't want him to leave me!"

"He knew what he was doing, Abi," I told her again. "He was taking advantage of you. He knew better. You didn't and that is not your fault!"

"How could I not have known better? Why didn't I see through him? Was I so easy?"

I did not know how to tell her to fight the self-loathing. How could I when I did not know how to fight it myself?

"I am like the worst person in the world!" She went on angrily. "I should feel bad about losing the baby but...I'm so relieved. Like, I didn't feel anything for it at all. What does that make me? What kind of mother would I have been?

Am I such a bad person? I couldn't bear the thought of having a baby that would grow up to be as lonely and miserable as me."

We were silent for a bit before Fola said, "You're not a bad person, Abi. You're like the rest of us who make mistakes. Don't beat yourself up. I hate to be cliché but you're going to move on and we're going to help you do that. You're not alone."

"I'm so thoughtless!" Abi cried. "I haven't asked you how you've been, Fola!"

"I'm hanging in there." Fola smiled. "Trying to move on too as best as I can."

"How about you, Lara? How is the medication therapy going?"

Uh-oh. Fola was going to flip her lid at being kept in the dark.

"What medication therapy?" Fola turned to me. "What are you on meds for, Lara?"

"Yeah, um..."

"Lara, I'm sorry!" Abi winced. "I thought you'd have told her if you'd told me."

"Told me what? What is up with us keeping secrets from each other? When did that start?"

Abi and I looked at her, abashed.

"Will you tell me what's going on? What medication therapy is she talking about, Lara?" Fola persisted.

"I'm in treatment for hepatitis B, Fola," I answered in a clipped tone

"You are what...?" She exclaimed, aghast. "I don't...how did you get that? And why am I just finding out?"

"See, I—"

"How could you have kept something this big a deal away from me?"

"I was—" I tried again, searching wildly for an excuse that would not be as insensitive as pointing out the obvious—that she had had other things to worry about.

She did not give me enough time. "Isn't this wonderful? My daddy's dead, Abi's lost her baby and you have...whatever you call it! God knows what Bibs will come up with to top all that!" Fola spat.

"Whoa, and I thought I was the one with the monopoly on speaking without thinking first!" I said wryly.

"Fine, that was a lot but really, what is going on with us? When did we start keeping stuff from one another? Look at the crazy stuff we've been going through and yet, we're so far apart when we need each other the most. You won't talk to me, Abi won't talk to you, I won't talk to Abi, and Bibs won't talk to any one of us! This is not how our friendship works, guys!"

"You're right." I agreed. "And I'm sorry I didn't tell you earlier. It's been a bit of a shock and I've been having a hard time dealing. I only just told Abi about it the other day. Besides, you've had enough to deal with, Fola, come on."

"Fair enough. But how is the therapy, did I hear that right, how's it going?" Fola asked worriedly.

"Well, I started my medications and things are looking up, the doctor says. The side effects of the meds are wearing off, which is good because those were a pain but yeah...I'm on my way to better, thank you for caring. Again, I'm sorry I didn't tell you earlier."

"What causes it? Do you know how you got it or...?" Fola asked.

"We aren't sure," I answered in a rush, "but you should know that I did stupidly experiment with drugs once. It was just the one time, but I probably used an unsterilized needle, so I guess once was enough."

Don't shed a flipping tear, I warned myself. I held my breath and blinked back the tears. I could see the questions in their eyes, and I wanted so much to answer them and tell them what had driven me to the brink.

I wanted to tell them about James, the loving stepfather turned sick pervert who deserved to die a horrible death a hundred times over. I wanted to tell them how he had abused my mother and I's trust, how he had made me a stranger in my home, a stranger to myself as I embarked on crazy, reckless stunts in a dire attempt to alert someone, anyone, that something was horribly wrong.

I wanted to tell them how ashamed I was—ashamed of me, ashamed of him, ashamed that it had happened, ashamed that I had let it happen. I wanted to let them know that like Abi, I could not help the self-loathing because I felt I should have put my foot down and spoken up sooner.

I wanted badly to share all of this with my best friends, but the words were stuck in my throat. After all this time, I was too afraid to admit to anyone that I had failed myself by being weak at a time I should have been stronger.

The truth was I had pretended for so long to be the damaged girl *on purpose* rather than admit that I had been given no choice not to be. Admitting that horrible truth meant that everyone, including me, would see right through the tough, invulnerable façade I had put on most of my life. If I were forced to put aside that façade, I was afraid I would not know the person behind it. I was afraid I would not know who I was.

So, I blinked away the threatening tears and smirked. "I was just being an idiot, you know, experimenting with stuff like that for a laugh. It was dumb of me and look who's paying for it now! It is what it is."

We fell silent after that.

"Do you guys want to get in the bed with me?" Abi asked suddenly. We stared at her in surprise, and then laughing, Fola and I squeezed in with her, taking care not to jolt her.

There was hardly enough space for the three of us, not surprising given that the bed was made for one, but Fola and I held on to the edges of the bed for dear life, Abi sandwiched between us.

"Guys, I hate to be the Debbie Downer, but our friendship is kind of falling apart along with everything else," Fola said when we had found a shaky balance.

"Knowing that I have you guys is part of what has kept me going during all the craziness and I don't want to lose that," she explained, "and yet, I feel it happening. We used to be able to tell each other everything and now, I'm beginning to think that we never even knew each other to start with."

"I guess friendship takes more work than we have assumed. We have to make a promise to do better," Abi said.

"We will do better. We're already doing better by having this conversation," I added.

"That is true," Abi agreed.

"Ugh!" Fola groaned. "Why does bad stuff happen to good people? This is not how I pictured our last year together."

"Do you know I was thinking about that earlier today and I sort of put my finger on it?" Abi answered, almost dreamily. "In my mind, each of us had a lesson that we needed to learn. Could it maybe that we had to go through these different experiences to learn those lessons? And if so, maybe once we've grasped the lessons, we'll be stronger for it and our friendship will be stronger for it. That is what I would like to think, anyway."

We reflected as her words floated over us, blanketing us with a conviction that everything was going to work out, that everything was going to be all right...in the end.

"Girl, if these are lessons, they are hard, and I say we all deserve As!" Fola said.

"Yeah, the As I didn't score in Physics and Math! Those exams were killer!" I joked.

The three of us cracked up.

"I love you guys," Abi said in a whisper. "Thank you for being here."

"As if we would rather be anywhere else, babe!" I snorted, the movement almost bumping me off the minuscule space I had claimed on the bed.

We lay on our backs on that small hospital bed, our hands linked, and our hearts connected.

"I wonder if Bibs would have been able to squeeze on to the bed if she was here," Fola said lazily. "We're barely hanging on."

"Yes, it doesn't feel complete without Bibs. I wish she were here," Abi said.

"Me too," Fola chimed in.

"Me three," I added, my eyes drifting shut. "Me three."

CHAPTER THIRTY
Bibs

...FAVORITE GAME WE LOVED to play when we were younger. It was a simple game where we would each take turns saying what we wanted to be when we grew up.

"When I grow up, I want to be a lawyer," she would say.

I would counter with, "When I grow up, I want to be a pilot."

Amina played it safe with her laundry list—a doctor, a lawyer, an engineer. I was more daring. I wanted to be a chef, an astronaut, a tattooist, a milliner, something exotic and different. That was then.

Amina is not here with me, so I'll play the game alone. What do I want to be now that I'm being forced to grow up?

That's easy. Now that it is time to grow up, the only thing I want to be is...free.

HERE I AM SITTING AT the dressing table, staring pensively at my reflection in the mirror, brushing my hair compulsively.

I have been waiting a suspenseful while for the other shoe to drop, and it has. At last, it has. I have played the last card I had left in the game and I have lost.

You see, with the calculated hope that he would grant me my petition when I summoned the courage to ask, I have dutifully been surrendering to Bamaiyi's attentions every night for the past couple of weeks.

Each night, I have stretched on the bed, cold and immobile, staring up at the ceiling and waiting for his nightmarish ministrations to be over.

Each night, when he collapsed heavily on me after draining his poison into me, I have listened to him whisper, *it'll get better. You'll enjoy it next time.*

Each time, I have ignored his whispers until he gave up trying to get a word out of me and left.

I wince now as the spikes of the brush tangle with the coils of my hair. Yes, I am still brushing.

As part of what I thought to be a shrewd plan, I stopped holing myself up in the room, to Bamaiyi's pleasure. I showed my face for the three meals of the day, all of which I ate in sullen silence.

The household had long since given up trying to befriend me, even the children. The children would bug me whenever they saw me moving moodily across the living room or they would saunter into my room for treats if my room door happened to be open. They did not do that anymore. They had been re-buffed one time too many.

These days, I could hardly look at Abu, much less hold him. I knew I was wrong to believe it, but I could not stop myself from thinking that if he had never been born, Bamaiyi would have been less able to strong-arm me into re-turning.

He would toddle up to me the few instances I let him spot me, squealing my name joyfully. Sometimes, I rushed away before he could reach me, my heart breaking as I did so. Other times, I would run and scoop him up into a too-tight hug until he squirmed in protest. I would carry him to my room then and sing to him until he fell asleep.

But back to my plan now. It was simple—I wanted, no, I *needed* Bamaiyi to let me out. The holidays were almost over, you see. Another school term was about to commence after the weekend. I had to go back to school then. If I did not, I was going to go mad.

I could not continue to be locked up in this house and in my mind. I had to get out and breathe the gratifying, unrestricted air of freedom, but I had to play nice for that to happen. I had to play nice so Bamaiyi would let me go back to school and my friends. I missed my friends. I needed my friends.

I missed Dimeji too, but he was a distant memory, one that made me smile whenever he crossed my mind. If I got to see him again, I would not let him back in. I would not tell him again how much I loved him. He deserved better than me. He deserved better than a used and broken girl.

I wince again as I brush harder. Yes, I am still brushing. It is going to be a long night, you see.

Two nights ago, I had bitten the bullet after over two long, tortuous weeks of grinning and bearing it.

I had even managed a sickly smile when Bamaiyi came into my room and undressed. I remained motionless on the bed, willing him to hurry up and when he rolled over, I did not clam up as usual.

Instead, I had asked hesitantly, "How was your day, sir?"

He started in surprise, transparently surprised that I was addressing him and almost pleasantly at that.

"It was a good one," he answered uncertainly as though unsure of how much to tell me. "Business was good, *na gode Allah*."

"*Na gode Allah*," I said, echoing his thanks to God. My heart pounded as I geared up to make my request.

"Can I ask my husband a favor?" I had simpered after a beat, spurred on by the thought of continuing captivity.

"Anything that will make you happy," he had replied after a pause.

"C-c-can I go back to school?"

"School?"

"Y-yes, school starts next week."

I watched him apprehensively as he started to slip on his clothes, holding my breath for his answer.

Finally, he had looked up and said crisply, "No."

"N-no?" I refused to accept that as his final answer.

"I said no!"

That was it? After the hard work I had put into playing along the past weeks?

I sat up in frustration. "What do you mean by no? Do you seriously want me to spend the rest of my life here in this house doing nothing?"

He stood up to leave. "I said no and that is final! What is the matter with you? Your father didn't warn me that you were spoiled rotten. Listen to me, you're not going back to school, not now, not ever! The sooner you get that into your thick skull, the better for you! You're now a married woman. You're a wife and a mother and you better start behaving like one!"

"Why don't you send me back to my father if I'm not what you planned for? Why are you bent on ruining my life?" I cried.

"I can see now that you've been taking my patience for granted. Lebiba, the next time you try my patience, I will show you how a husband puts his wife in her place. You better mind yourself and know your place. Know your place! *Mu kwana lafiya.*"

Shaking, I had watched him storm out with that final and abrupt goodnight. That had been two nights ago—Friday.

Last night, when Hadiza had come to tell me that I had a caller holding on the landline, I had ignored her, thinking it was my mother again. Hajia had maintained the habit, possibly out of guilt, of showing up or calling almost every day under the pretext of making sure Abu was comfortable.

After seconds of deliberation, I had decided to go take the call, itching for the chance to take out some of my frustration on someone else.

"Hello," I had said shortly as I picked up the call.

"Bibs, it's me!"

Lara!

My helplessness had streamed to the surface when I heard my best friend's voice and I had let out a piteous wail.

"Bibs!" I heard Lara cry in alarm. "What is wrong? What's going on? Where are you?"

I held the receiver and squalled inconsolably.

"Bibs, please stop!" She pleaded.

"I'm sorry!" I choked out at last. "I'm just so happy to hear from you!"

"I'm happy to hear your voice too! I've been so worried about you! I've been trying to get a hold of you for ages, but your cell has been off. I finally got a hold of your mom yesterday and she gave me this number to call you on, but she wouldn't tell me where you were or what has been going on. What *is* going on? Where are you?"

"I...I am at a relative's." I could not bear to tell her the truth.

"I see." She knew I was lying. "When are you coming home?"

"I-I don't know...yet."

"You can talk to me, Bibs. It won't do you any good to keep it in. Now, tell me, what is really going on?"

"Lara, it's nothing. I upset my father and he sent me here for a while, but I can't talk about it right now."

"I get it. Dimeji has been asking for you too. He hasn't been able to reach you either."

I felt my heart flutter. "How is he?"

"He's good but he's been super worried about you. We've all been. Do you want me to give him this number so he can call? He desperately wants to talk to you."

There was no way I could have allowed Dimeji to call me here. It would have been tantamount to adding fuel to the raging fire.

"No!" I told her firmly. "I-I'll call him later. How are Fola and Abi?"

"They are...good." She hesitated. "Actually, they would like to tell you that for themselves. Hang on, they want to say hello."

I heard her fiddle around as she switched to speaker phone mode.

"Bibs, can you hear us?"

"Bibs, we've missed you!"

"Where on earth did you disappear to, this babe?"

I began to sob again as the three voices filtered loudly through the receiver.

"I've missed you guys too!" I cried. They had sounded thrilled to hear me, almost as thrilled as I had been to hear them. I laughed through my tears as they each fought for control of the phone.

After a round of exclamations and cries, Lara had turned her speakerphone off so that it was me and her again.

"Bibs, do you remember what I told you that day?" she asked. I knew in a flash the day she was referring to. It was the day she had seen my wounds—the self-inflicted physical wounds on my thighs and the involuntary emotional wounds in my eyes.

"I told you I'd always be here for you whenever you were ready to talk. Don't ever forget that I'm always, *always* going to be here. If you're not ready to talk today, then I'll ask tomorrow and if not then, I'll ask the day after that, and the day after that, and the day after that until you are ready. Do you hear me?" she said fiercely.

The love and concern in her voice had felt like a knife neatly slicing my heart in two. It had put me to shame and had made up my mind for me. I had known then with a deadly certainty the way out.

"I hear you. It's all good." I had smiled, knowing she could not see but hoping she could tell from my voice.

"Good! I love you. We love you!"

"I love you guys too."

"Awesome! So, we'll see you in school on Monday?"

I closed my eyes against the heartache her words created and replied, my voice almost breaking. "Yes, see you in school on Monday."

After she had rung off, I had held onto the receiver, not wanting to let go, as though a part of me thought that by holding on, I could somehow go along with her, with them. It was the part of me that had not given up yet, the part of me that yearned for freedom.

Later that night, I had scrounged around for some paper and a pen and written a letter. Inserting the completed letter in an envelope, I had licked it shut and inserted it inside the drawer beneath my dressing table, knowing it would wait there until someone thought to deliver it for me.

See you in school on Monday. That had been last night—Saturday.

Here I am now sitting at the dressing table, staring pensively at my reflection in the mirror. I am no longer brushing my hair, but I am nowhere near done with the night's ritual. Not yet.

I amble to the bathroom to run the water for a bath. No long, hot shower where I scrub myself raw, no, not tonight. A long, warm bath is in order.

I slowly undress as the water fills the tub. Once the tub is full, I twist the tap close and test the water. It has to be warm enough—not too hot, not too cold. Satisfied, I sink into the warm water, exhaling in bliss. It feels like coming home.

I have made no secret of how much I love the water. I can stay in the shower for hours. I can walk miles in the rain if allowed. The sensation of water against my skin is soul-cleansing. Who knows, I might have been a mermaid in another life.

I lean over now and dip my head into the bathwater until my hair is thoroughly soaked and I massage my hands through the thick, curly mass.

As the water moves over my body, I feel everything fall away—the shame, the hurt, the rage, the helplessness. They are washed away as usual by the water but tonight, they will not ever be coming back.

I stretch and reach for the new razor, perched on the edge of the tub, enclosed in a tiny, pretty paper envelope. The ugliest things come wrapped in the prettiest packages, like me.

You've seen this before, you think disgustedly as I unwrap the razor.

But this time, you are wrong, you will see.

This time, I am doing it different.

This time, the edge of the razor is not going left to right. The edge of the razor is going up and down, up and down, up and down. *Down the river, not across the stream.*

This time, I am doing it for keeps, you see.

I stifle a gasp as the blood rushes furiously to the surface of the haggard gashes on both my wrists.

It is agony, sheer agony. It is the most pain I have felt in my life and I have felt a lot. I am almost tempted to jump out of the tub, but I do not.

It's all good, Lebiba, I tell myself. *It's all good.*

I exhale triumphantly as I lose the will to fight. I have been in a lifelong struggle for control, you see, but I am through with it. I have been fighting for so long but no more.

This way, I win. I wrestle back control from the usurpers. They have written my story for me long enough. I am the author now. The story is mine and will remain mine alone.

Light-headed, I lean back, my hands submerged, and I chew at my lips as the now tepid bathwater changes color.

It's all good, Lebiba, I tell myself again. *It will be good.*

Sure enough, a chill slowly replaces the pain, and I start to tremble. Before long, even the chill is gone, and everything goes numb. To my burgeoning relief, I can no longer feel anything. Do you understand the magnitude of that, that I feel *nothing*?

I have felt a wide host of emotions in my lifetime—fear, loneliness, pain, joy, desire, you name it—but now, in this moment, I feel nothing. Could this be that strange thing they call peace?

I close my eyes and frown at the thought of the chaos I will leave behind. It is only a fleeting thought before I pivot to savor my memories.

I read once that when a life hangs in the balance, hovering between life and death, the soul's final act is to replay its most precious memories.

Is my life hanging in the balance now? I wonder as memories replay through my head like a slideshow—the night my son was born, the day he sprouted his first tooth, the first word he uttered which was a mangled version of my name, the riotous moments I have shared with my best friends, discovering love and touch with Dimeji.

I am watching the memories flash through my head in rapid succession, as though they belong to someone else and I am an intruder at best, but these are my memories. These are my most precious memories, you see.

My final memory is of my girls, of the first time we four sat on the concrete ledge under the gum tree and claimed it as our territory.

"Kookaburra sits in the old gum tree,
Merry, merry king of the bush is he.
Laugh, Kookaburra, laugh,
Kookaburra, gay your life must be!"

The memory of my best friends and I raucously chanting that old rhyme under our very own old gum tree makes me smile and now, tears sting the back of my aching eyes.

Lara.

Fola.

Abi.

The best friends ever. I did not get to say goodbye.

I exhale shakily. I am weak. I am exhausted. I am tired. I am ready to let go. All I want now is to...sleep. And so, I do.

I close my eyes and I sleep.

I close my eyes, I sleep, and I dream.

I dream of four birds perched at the top of an old gum tree.

Suddenly, one soars gleefully from the tree into the open skies.

It bursts into its unmistakable call—an uncannily loud, echoing human laughter—as it soars higher and higher and higher towards freedom.

Not until the three birds left behind burst into answering calls of high-pitched laughter, do I realize that the sole laughing bird bound for freedom...is me.

"...Laugh, Kookaburra, laugh.
Kookaburra, gay your life must be!"

FOR AS LONG AS THEY could remember, the four girls had always sat on the concrete ledge under the gum tree. There had never been any contention about the seating arrangement either—Lebiba on the right side, Abi on the left, and Lara and Fola sandwiched in between the two. The fit was tight but right.

Now, three girls sat on the concrete ledge under the gum tree with an empty space on the right. It was an empty space as empty as their hearts and there was no one there to fill it up.

IT CALLED TO MIND THE day in the hospital when the three of us had barely managed to squeeze onto Abi's small hospital bed.

One of us had wondered aloud if Bibs would have been able to squeeze in and hold on too. Here was our answer.

There was no one sitting on the right side of the concrete ledge under the gum tree. It was an empty space as empty as our hearts and there was no one there to fill it up.

EPILOGUE
Lara

AT EIGHTEEN, MY FRIENDS and I struck everyone as your typical, run-of-the-mill teenagers—the invincible sort who thought the world their very own oyster, you know, who thought they knew everything there was to know about themselves, about each other, about everyone else around them, about life.

That had been once upon our childhood. That had been before the prettily embroidered stories of our individual lives ripped apart at the seams. That had been when we believed in the happily ever after.

But you know what? Even now. Yes, even now. We still believe.

"...AND IN CONCLUSION, I would like to thank my dearest friends, my best friends, my sisters. Without them, the inspiration to bring this dream to life today would have been null and void. Fola, Abi and Bibs, I love you guys and *this*...this is for us."

A thunderous standing ovation follows the end of my short but moving speech. I blink back tears, beaming at the sizable audience who have turned out in unanticipated numbers to support what is the result of three years of hard work by my colleagues and me.

The fruit of our labor is a new shelter for women and children looking for a temporary sanctuary. Sponsored by the private law firm I work for, in partnership with the Lagos State Government, the governor herself, Aderayo Fadejo, has made an appearance to cut the red tape and unveil the building.

My eyes meet the twin grins of understanding and pride at the front of the audience. My girls have made it here and as I told everyone seconds ago, this triumph was for us.

I must be frank—it has taken me years of therapy to understand and acknowledge that my three friends and I had been abused, albeit some more subtly than the others.

We had suffered the abuse of our innocence and trust by those we had held dear to us—I by my stepfather, Fola by her father, Abi by the man she thought to be her first love, and Bibs by almost everyone in her life.

We had been abused and despite our education, our exposure, and our strong friendship, we had suffered in deadly silence. We had shared with one another everything but the stories of how our childhood had been stolen and perverted by those we had entrusted them to.

It made me pause and think. If we, despite the buffer our friendship provided, could suffer so in silence, how much more those with no support system of their own? If we, as seemingly privileged as we had been, had been unable to fight back against our abusers, how much less those who were not as privileged?

The heavy thought weighed on me. Nobody should have to suffer alone. Nobody should have to suffer in silence. I had seen and experienced firsthand how suffering alone and in silence led the abused to self-abuse

I did not want to accept that there was no recourse for the abused among us. I envisioned a safe place where women and children could seek repose.

A safe place where they could pause long enough to lick their wounds, unburden themselves of the secrets they had held to themselves too long, and heal.

A safe space where they could be bold enough to rebuke the lies that they had told to protect their abusers.

A safe space where they could be strong enough to break down the walls that they had built to protect their vulnerability.

A safe space where they could be audacious enough to fight back against the culture of silence and complacency that fostered their abuse.

A safe space where they could be powerful enough to fight for their freedom and more importantly, win.

I had harped on and on about my vision until one day, Ladi, my husband, had challenged me. *Why don't you do something about it?* He had asked.

And I had thought to myself, *why not?*

For two long years, I had worked hard, in addition to my day job, to secure the sponsorship and infrastructure needed to build and manage a non-profit platform that would provide temporary physical and emotional support to women and children fleeing domestic violence and abuse. My team and I had designed the platform to also provide prevention and education programs that would help reduce the incidence of domestic violence, sexual assault, and child abuse.

Securing the sponsorship had been easier said than done. Given the shoddy maintenance culture around us, many were skeptical that such a shelter could be built and managed effectively and transparently. Others thought the shelter an excuse to encourage open rebellion and insubordination.

"You want our children to be calling the authorities on their parents like they do abroad? What nonsense!" That had been one of several ignorant comments directed at me, this by a querulous female member of the Lagos State House of Representatives confirming yet again that she had more education than common sense.

My team and I had surged on, undaunted. In the third year, having gathered a handful of individual and corporate sponsors, we had struck gold.

The governor had reached out, having heard of our efforts through a mutual contact. She had gotten her administration to throw its weight behind the project without further ado.

And now, here we were today, our efforts brought to fruition! At last, there was hope, hope for those who needed to turn their pain to strength like my friends and I had done.

We did not all make it, as you already know. I often think back to that fateful day at the hospital when Fola and I had squeezed onto Abi's narrow hospital bed, blissfully and regrettably unaware the fourth member of our quartet had been in so much pain that she would opt for suicide as the way out.

To this day, I remember Fola's dispirited query then about why bad things happened to good people. Abi's astute response had struck an eerie chord. In fact, Fola had brought it up the first time the three of us had met up in London—the first time we had been reunited since graduating from Gatesbridge six years earlier.

I was halfway through law school in D.C. then, slaving through myriads and myriads of wordy tomes, Abi had recently graduated from the American University of Yola, and Fola was working in Liverpool and simultaneously completing her part-time MBA program.

It had been a chilly afternoon and we had huddled up on a couch on the second level of Starbucks, catching up and exclaiming excitedly about how much we had each changed.

Midway through our conversation, Fola had said quietly, "Abi, do you remember what you said that day at the hospital? About each of us having a lesson to learn and how we were maybe going through our different experiences to learn those lessons and be stronger for them? I was thinking the other day how right you turned out to be."

Abi and I had murmured in acquiescence as she went on, "For my part, I like to think that I'm not as narrow-minded and judgmental as I used to be. Nothing is black or white to me, it's all shades of gray."

"Ah, I'd forgotten I ever said that!" Abi laughed nervously. "But you're right. I did learn a thing or two. For one thing, men are scum!"

We had laughed and snapped our fingers in assent.

"But on a serious note," Abi had continued, "I'm not as impulsive or quick to jump into things. I don't take everything at face value anymore. Oh, and I don't think I'm as stupid as I was before!"

"Abi, you were never stupid!" Fola objected.

"Girl, I was *o*! I'm not as stupid so don't get worked up, love! But see, I find it very difficult to trust anyone."

Fola nodded. "I can relate to that."

"What about you, Lara?" Abi turned to me.

"Well," I said uncertainly, "I would say that I'm perhaps less cynical about life, although I will tell you law school is trying its best to make me maintain status quo! And yo, going through the dreaded Hep B made me realize that every action of mine has a consequence that might not necessarily show up right away and so, I try to be thoughtful about my decisions now."

That had been the tone of our conversation for the rest of the evening—talking about lessons learned. Somehow, we had inadvertently turned out the better for everything that had happened to us although some scars were yet to heal.

Therapy had been a significant part of my healing process as I mentioned earlier. For the first time, I had opened up about James to someone else, worked through my feelings of shame, self-disgust, and misdirected anger, and altogether, found some closure.

Part of that closure had included confiding in my family. My coming clean had, of course, caused dissent and had left Mom critically blaming herself, Dad blaming Mom, my brothers blaming them both, etcetera, but they had been able to put the blame aside to rally around me.

Like I had told my friends, I had also become much more sensitive, having made it a conscious habit to be thoughtful about what I said or did before I said or did it. Having a daughter did that to you.

Having a daughter had also made me fearful. I saw sexual predators everywhere—Ladi's first cousin once-removed, the security guard at the gatehouse, the houseboy next door, you get the picture. Anyone, male or female, in the vicinity of my daughter had to be thoroughly vetted. I lived with an overly heightened sense of awareness. That was my scar.

Fola had bounced back to her old self, albeit a much-improved version as I would always tell her cheekily. She was her loud, boisterous self but much softer around the edges, not as quick to judge or criticize people including those below her station as she was once wont to do.

Her mom had stuck to her word and walked away from everything her dad had left. Mrs. Adeyemi had easily stepped into the void that her husband's death had created, and she and her children were closer than before.

At first, Fola had complained incessantly that her mother was lonely, but she had been almost through with college when to her relief, her mom had met and remarried a friend of an old friend.

Fola herself was engaged but prior to that, had gone through an extraordinarily long chain of relationships, loving and leaving before she could get hurt. Even now she was planning her wedding, she would call me from time to time to complain about cold feet. That was her scar.

Abi was the sweet, talkative, and sensitive person she had always been but with one fundamental difference—she was now unrepentantly cynical.

Without blinking twice, she had cut her father out of her life for refusing to pay her university fees. He was begging to be a part of her life now, the irony. Things were better with her mother. They were no longer bitter enemies, more like familiar strangers.

When she had gotten married two years ago, I had asked if she felt concerned about the age difference between her husband and herself—a whopping sixteen years.

"Ah no, Lara!" She had giggled. "It's safer that way *o*! These older men have done all the nonsense they need to do. They've gotten it out of their system. That is the way I like it because I don't want to spend my life looking over my husband's shoulders."

That was the scar Jimi had left, a perpetual lack of trust in the capricious male species. And no, she had never seen or heard from him since their last conversation, if we could call it that, where she had learned about his fiancée.

And then, there was Bibs. Twelve years and I still got a lump in my throat whenever I remembered the friend I would never see again.

After the initial shock and grief, I had been angry, so angry. For one, I had been angry at Bibs. I had wanted to be there for her and had told her that repeatedly, but she had never let me. Why had she not talked to me, to us? Why had she not let us in? How could she have chosen to leave us without any warning? I had been angry at her for not being stronger.

I had also been angry at myself. The last time I had seen her in person, we had parted on a sour note. I had accused her of being too wrapped up in Dimeji at the expense of us, her friends. I had berated her for being selfish, but little had I known then that she had found out the day before that she was being shipped off to her rapist.

What sort of lousy friend had I been to not have realized that my presumed best friend had been in such unbearable pain? There had been signs that I had ignored. I had seen her cuts. Why had I not spoken up in time? Why had I not paid more attention? I had been angry at myself for failing her.

I had been even angrier at the system. What good were parents we could not tell anything? What good was a guidance counselor who stared at you blankly like you were the sole architect of every bad thing that happened to you? What good was a culture that responded so negatively to issues of mental and emotional health?

Two weeks after the funeral, Bibs' mother had sent over a package to my house—a sealed letter addressed to me from Bibs. It had been found in the drawer of her dressing table when her things were being cleared away.

I had read the letter in increasing shock and repulsion, taking in the details of her rape by a family friend she had been betrothed to, the pregnancy that had resulted from her rape, the birth of Abu, and her father's cruel decision to send her and Abu back to the house of this same rapist.

I had cried myself to sleep every night for a week with the same question on my mind—how had she gone through all of it alone and for so long?

In her letter, Bibs had left the decision of telling the others her story to me and I had done so, not right away. I had eventually told them the weekend we had spent together in London, and after their initial outrage, we had had a good cry about the cruelty of it all.

It was maddening that the perpetrators of her abuse, like ours, had blithely gone on with their lives without a care in the world for the destruction they had left in their wake.

Nevertheless, some good had come out of it in the end. Bibs' mother had ultimately honored her daughter by fighting harder than a wounded lioness (and in some way, she had been that) to win custody of her grandson from his father. She was raising him now with the true knowledge of who his mother was. I was in touch with her and more frequently with Abu.

In my opinion, our theory of lessons learned falls through when we apply it to Bibs. I get emotionally riled up when I think about the tragedies she endured. What lessons could she have learned from those?

My mother says sometimes that God will never give you anything more than you can bear. Well, why had God not thought to turn off the pressure before Bibs slit her wrists and died? That is what I think when I am angry.

But more often, I am thankful.

I am thankful for the lifetime of memories I got to build and share with her.

I am thankful for the times she held my hand though I turned out to be so inept in holding hers.

I am thankful for her eager ears, her soft words, and her uncanny way of brokering peace for others as much as peace eluded her.

I am thankful for the warm hugs and kisses she would force on my cheeks.

I am thankful for the memory of her shy, beautiful smile engraved in my head and my heart.

I am thankful she left her essence in her beautiful boy. Abu, my self-declared godson, is fifteen now.

Most of all, I am thankful because she is the reason my vision has come alive today. I strove hard to see it come true for her.

I constantly wonder what it would be like if she was here with us today. What would the story of her life have been if she had, like the rest of us, wrested back her childhood from those who had stolen it away?

Sadly, she never got the chance to do that. So here we are, doing it for her. We are doing it for the *thousands* of Bibs out there. She may have lost the battle, but this is us, winning the war on her behalf.

I smile now and descend from the podium to where my family, friends, and well-wishers are waiting to congratulate me.

There is Mom and Dad, still separated but good friends, and my two brothers who, like me, have both moved back to Nigeria with their families and are doing successfully.

There is Fola. She is cheesing so hard; her dimples appear to be drilling holes in both cheeks. She waves excitedly as I approach, her ridiculously huge engagement ring flashing.

You will never believe who she is engaged to. Tunji! Yes, the same old Tunji! They had lost contact after Gatesbridge, but then had run into each other a couple of years later and discovered for themselves that old feelings sometimes did die hard.

Due to his crazy work schedule, he was unfortunately unable to make the trip to Nigeria from Liverpool where they both live. The wedding is in a couple of months, however, so I will see him then.

There is Abi, glowing prettily, her baby bump so huge and far distended she might topple over any second. Her husband, apparently wary of that same fact, is gently supporting her lower back with his hand.

He shoots me a cheeky grin as I wink at him and mouth noiselessly, "Chief, Chief!" He has insisted that I call him by his first name, Michael, but I can't find it in me to comply with the old man.

It is Abi's first child after trying for years. It was such a relief for her when she found out that she was pregnant. She had once admitted to me that she agonized about her past abortion attempt possibly having ruined her chances of ever getting pregnant. Happily, that turned out to be nonsense!

There is Ladi. Ladi is my husband, has been for four years running, and will be forever and ever, so help us, God. Ha. I will spare you the gushing because he does have a disgusting ability to make me gush like I am doing right now.

I met him when he was an annoying client that a colleague was working on a case for. Little did I envisage then that he would proceed to fall in love with me and persuade me to reciprocate in kind.

If you were wondering about Manny, by the way, we had broken up after he left for college. He is unmarried but he does have two adorable kids. He remains a good friend of mine and we speak often.

I light up as my eighteen-month old daughter, Abiola—everyone calls her Bibi—spots me and begins to struggle in her dad's arms, reaching for me to carry her, with a partly-toothless smile across her face.

It had taken sixteen agonizing hours of labor to get her out much to her father's extreme dismay but once she had popped right out and let out her first wail, it had made every hour worth it.

I have not told Ladi my suspicion about a little brother being on the way. He has yet to recover from the last time. Ha.

So yes, we are all here. Everyone is here. Everyone...even Bibs.

I am not being whimsical now. I swear I can feel her here too, amid this hour of victory.

As if for proof, I hear a faint whisper in my ear.

Good, I think I hear her say. *It's all good.*

She would say that all the time.

Yes, Lebiba, it is good. It is all good.

Acknowledgements

I WROTE MY FIRST DRAFT of Once Upon Our Childhood at fourteen. It was endearing (to me, anyway) fan fiction inspired by Enid Blyton's Mallory Towers and so, you must understand why that version will remain stashed away, never to be revealed.

Time and experience have helped refine that beguiling draft which I am releasing as a much belated and imperfect pet project, thanks to the relentless push of my first readers.

To every reader of this book, both old and new, I hope you fall in love with the girls as much as I did. May you continue to discover worlds via words.

To the motley crew of objective and impartial reviewers who helped edit my manuscript, shared constructive criticism, and offered invaluable advice in more ways than one, I owe you a great debt, thank you.

To the loyal cohort who tore through many, sometimes painful, revisions of this story, who led me to amazing contacts, and who pushed me to *just get it out*, thank you for not giving up.

To Dee, thank you for being the best friend (sorry you have to share, GC!) in our journeys then, now, and yet to come. You are the *Peak* to my *Milo*.

To Dad and Mama, thank you for believing in me always and blessing every single one of my dreams with unwavering support. I love you both so much.

To Lara, Fola, Abi and Bibs, I loved every minute of writing your stories. Thank you for letting me laugh and cry along with each of you as my pen brought you to life.

Finally, to the Author and Finisher of my faith...*You* are good.

About the Author

AN ONLY CHILD UNTIL a sister popped up five years later; Lara Brown spent those solo years voraciously reading every book she could lay her hands on. Books have remained a fascination for her and over the years, she has authored various unpublished stories and poems.

Her day job centers around creating meaningful experiences in the workplace. She hopes to create more time for her writing amidst work, travel, and of course, more books.

Once Upon Our Childhood is her first published work.

Connect with Me

Subscribe to my blog: Worlds via Words[1]
Send me a note: LaraBrown@worldsviawords.com
Follow me on Twitter: @worldsviawords[2]

---

1. https://worldsviawords.com

2. https://twitter.com/worldsviawords

Helpline

IF YOU OR SOMEONE YOU know is thinking about suicide or considering self-harm, please get help. Call the Nigerian Suicide Prevention Initiative - NSPI Counseling Center at 234-806-210-6493 or send a note to sspinitiative@gmail.com.

Other Helpful Resources

Domestic And Sexual Violence Response Team – DSVRT, Lagos State
http://www.dsvrtlagos.org/

Stand To End Rape (S.T.E.R) Initiative
http://standtoendrape.org/

Mirabel Centre (SARC)
http://mirabelcentre.org/

Women At Risk International Foundation – WARIF
https://warifng.org/

Hands OFF!
https://www.handsoffinitiative.org/